Ash's look seared Tori and she shifted in her seat. It wasn't just relief she felt. Her emotions were complex and she found herself growing nervous all over again.

The longer she sat with him, the more she realized how little she knew about Ash, despite the way her body hummed with awareness. He seemed light-years away from the stoic man with whom she'd shared intimacies in the desert.

She couldn't imagine—

No, that was wrong. She *could* imagine all too easily the urge to be with him again. The realization sent heat spiraling through her middle and surging up her throat to scald her cheeks.

Yet it wasn't sexual awareness stretching her nerves tight. It was apprehension. For she knew next to nothing about him. His life, hopes, expectations. How he'd react when faced with what she had to tell him.

For a craven moment she wondered if she could avoid that. It would be taking a giant step into the unknown.

But it had to be done. She moistened her lips, ready to speak, but he was too fast for her.

"So, Tori. Or should I call you Victoria?" He leaned closer, his black-as-night gaze pinioning her to the seat. "Are you going to tell me about my son?"

Secret Heirs of Billionaires

There are some things money can't buy...

Living life at lightning pace, these magnates are no strangers to stakes at their highest. It seems they've got it all... That is, until they find out that there's an unplanned item to add to their list of accomplishments!

Achieved:

1. Successful business empire.

2. Beautiful women in their bed.

3. *An heir to bear their name?*

Though every billionaire needs to leave his legacy in safe hands, discovering a secret heir shakes up the carefully orchestrated plan in more ways than one!

Uncover their secrets in:

The Sheikh's Secret Baby by Sharon Kendrick

The Sicilian's Secret Son by Angela Bissell

Claimed for the Sheikh's Shock Son by Carol Marinelli

Shock Heir for the King by Clare Connelly

Demanding His Hidden Heir by Jackie Ashenden

The Maid's Spanish Secret by Dani Collins

Look out for more stories in the
Secret Heirs of Billionaires series coming soon!

Annie West

SHEIKH'S ROYAL BABY REVELATION

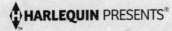 **HARLEQUIN** PRESENTS®

Recycling programs for this product may not exist in your area.

ISBN-13: 978-1-335-47859-7

Sheikh's Royal Baby Revelation

First North American publication 2019

Copyright © 2019 by Annie West

Printed in U.S.A.

www.Harlequin.com

Growing up near the beach, **Annie West** spent lots of time observing tall, burnished lifeguards—early research! Now she spends her days fantasizing about gorgeous men and their love lives. Annie has been a reader all her life. She also loves travel, long walks, good company and great food. You can contact her at annie@annie-west.com or via PO Box 1041, Warners Bay, NSW 2282, Australia.

Books by Annie West

Harlequin Presents

Seducing His Enemy's Daughter
Inherited for the Royal Bed
Her Forgotten Lover's Heir
The Greek's Forbidden Innocent

One Night With Consequences

Contracted for the Petrakis Heir
A Vow to Secure His Legacy

Secret Heirs of Billionaires

The Desert King's Secret Heir

Passion in Paradise

Wedding Night Reunion in Greece

The Princess Seductions

His Majesty's Temporary Bride
The Greek's Forbidden Princess

Visit the Author Profile page
at Harlequin.com for more titles.

For the late-night laughter and plotting
just when I needed it!

Thank you AA, Bron, Kandy, Shaz,
Denise, Rachel and Reeze.

CHAPTER ONE

ASHRAF WOKE TO the sound of a door slamming and the taste of blood in his mouth. Blood and dust.

He lay facedown, head and ribs burning with pain, the rest of him merely battered. Slowly he forced his eyelids open. He was in a dark room, lightened only by a spill of moonlight through a small, high window.

Then came rough voices using an obscure local dialect. Three men, he counted, walking away. He strained to hear over the merciless hammering in his head.

They'd kill him tomorrow. After Qadri arrived to enjoy the spectacle and pay them for the successful kidnap.

Ashraf gritted his jaw, ignoring the spike of pain in the back of his skull.

Of course Qadri was behind this. Who else would dare? The bandit leader had even begun to style himself as a provincial chief in the last years of Ashraf's father's rule.

The old Sheikh had moved slowly when dealing with problems in this remote province, the poorest and most backward in the country. He'd left Qadri alone as long as the bandit preyed only on his own people.

But Ashraf wasn't cut from the same cloth as his

father. The old Sheikh was dead and Ashraf had introduced changes that would see Qadri dispossessed.

He could expect no mercy from his captors.

Ashraf wasn't naïve enough to believe Qadri would negotiate his release. The man would fight for his fiefdom the only way he knew: with violence.

What better way to intimidate poor villagers than to execute the new Sheikh? To prove that modernisation and the rule of law had no place in the mountains that had only known Qadri's authority for two decades?

Ashraf cursed his eagerness to see a new irrigation project, accepting the invitation to ride out with just a local guide and a single bodyguard into an area that was supposedly now completely safe.

Safe!

His belly clenched as he thought of his bodyguard, Basim, thrown from his horse by a tripwire rigged between two boulders.

Ashraf had vaulted from his horse to go to him, only to be felled by attackers. There was little satisfaction in knowing they hadn't overpowered him easily.

Was Basim alive? Ashraf's gut clenched at the thought of his faithful guard abandoned where he'd fallen.

Fury scoured his belly. But fury wouldn't help now. Only cold calculation. He had to find a way out. Or a way to convey his location to those searching for him.

His father had always said he had the devil's own luck. It had been a sneering accusation, not a fond appraisal, but for the first time Ashraf found himself hoping the old man had been right. He could do with some luck. And the energy to move.

A slight scuffling broke his train of thought.

He wasn't alone.

Ashraf refused to lie there waiting for another knock-out blow.

Ignoring the pain that exploded through him at the movement, he rolled over and up onto his feet, only to stop abruptly, his right arm yanked back.

Spinning round, Ashraf discovered he was chained to a wall. Another turn, so swift his bruised head swam and pain seared his ribs. But with his back to the wall, his feet wide, he was ready to take on any assailant.

'Come on. Show yourself.'

Nothing. No movement. No sound.

Then, out of the darkness, something gleamed. Something pale that shone in the faint moonlight.

His guard was *blond*?

Ashraf blinked. It wasn't an hallucination.

Whoever it was, he wasn't local.

'Who are you?' He switched to French, then English, and heard an answering hiss of breath.

English, then.

The silence grew, ratcheting his tension higher.

'You don't know?' It was a whisper, as if the speaker feared being overheard.

Ashraf frowned. Had the blow to his head damaged his hearing? It couldn't be, yet it sounded like—

'You're a *woman*?'

'You're not one of them, then.' Her voice was flat, yet taut, as if produced by vocal cords under stress.

Stress he could understand.

'By "one of them" you mean…?'

'The men who brought me here. The men who…' Ashraf heard a shudder in her voice '…kidnapped me.'

'Definitely not one of them. They kidnapped me too.'

For which they'd pay. Ashraf had no intention of dying in what he guessed was a shepherd's hut, from the smell of livestock. Though the sturdy chain and handcuff indicated that the place was used for other, sinister purposes. He'd heard whispers that Qadri was involved in people-smuggling. That women in particular sometimes vanished without a trace, sold to unscrupulous buyers across the border.

The pale glow came closer. Ashraf saw her now. Silvery hair, pale skin and eyes that looked hollow in the shadows. She swallowed and he made out the convulsive movement of her throat. Calm overlying panic. At least she wasn't hysterical.

'Are you hurt?' he asked.

A tiny huff of amusement greeted his question. 'That's my line. You're the one who's bleeding.'

Ashraf looked down. Parting his torn shirt, he discovered a long cut, no longer bleeding. A knife wound, he guessed, but not deep.

'I'll live.'

Despite the playboy reputation Ashraf had once acquired, he'd done his time in the army. A stint which his father had ensured was tougher and more dangerous than usual. Ashraf knew enough about wounds to be sure he'd be alive when his executioner arrived tomorrow.

'How about you?'

Tori stared at him, wanting to laugh and cry at the same time.

Except tears wouldn't help. And she feared if she laughed it would turn into hysteria.

'Just scrapes and bruises.' She was lucky and she

knew it. Her jaw ached where she'd been backhanded across the face but that was the worst. Despite the hungry gleam she'd seen in her captors' eyes as they'd inspected her, they hadn't touched her except to subdue her and throw her in here.

Looking at this injured man, she trembled, thinking she'd got off lightly. So far.

He'd been unconscious when they'd dumped him on the dirt floor. Either he'd put up a mighty fight or they had a grudge against him to beat him up like that.

She hadn't had time to investigate how badly he was injured. His shirt was torn and stained and his head was bloody on one side. Even so, he stood tall. His ragged shirt hung from wide, straight shoulders and his dusty trousers clung to a horseman's thighs. He looked fit and powerful despite his injuries. Under the grime he had strong-boned features that she guessed might be handsome, or at least arresting.

Would she see him in daylight or would they come for her before that? Terror shuddered down her spine and turned her knees to jelly. Panic bit her insides as she imagined what was in store for her.

'Where are we?' Like her, the stranger kept his voice low, yet something about the smooth, deep note eased a fraction of the tension pinching her.

'Somewhere in the foothills. I couldn't see from the back of the van.' She wrapped her arms around her middle, remembering that trip, facing a grim stranger with a knife in his hand.

'There's a road?' The man before her pounced on that.

'Part of the way. I walked the last part blindfolded.'

Which was why her knees were rubbed raw after she'd stumbled and fallen time and again over uneven ground.

'Is there a guard at the door?'

'I don't think so.'

She'd heard the men talking as they walked away. Even so she crept to the door, peeking through the gap between it and the wall. No one. She moved along the wall but it was surprisingly solid, with no chinks to peer through.

As if it had been used as a prison before.

Tori thought of the heavy chain that secured her companion and her stomach curdled.

'There's a light further away. A campfire, I think. But no one here as far as I can tell.'

Why would they bother? The door was bolted. Her companion was chained and she didn't have as much as a pocket knife to use as a tool.

What wouldn't she give for her geologist's hammer right now? Designed for cracking rocks, the sharp end might prise open the chain and it would make an effective weapon.

'What are you doing?' He'd turned his back on her and she heard the rattle of metal links.

'Testing this chain.' There was a grunt, then a muffled oath.

She crossed to stand behind him. 'You won't pull it out,' she whispered. 'It's fixed securely. Believe me.'

'You've checked?' His hunched shoulders straightened as he lifted his head and turned around.

Suddenly he was closer than she'd expected, towering above her. Her hissed breath cut the thick silence.

Only hours ago she'd been grabbed by strangers: big men who'd overpowered her despite her frantic struggle. Fear curdled her belly anew and adrenaline pumped hard in her blood, freezing her to the spot.

Yet as she stiffened the man stepped back towards the wall. Giving her space.

Logic said he wasn't the enemy. Her abductors had kidnapped him too.

Tori sucked in oxygen and tried to steady her breathing. In the gloom she met his eyes. It was too dark to be sure but she'd swear she read sympathy in his face. And something else. Pity?

Because the fate of a woman abducted by violent men would be truly pitiful.

Tori stiffened her knees against the images she'd tried so hard not to picture. She couldn't afford to crack up now.

'Of course I checked.' She made herself concentrate on the conversation, not her fear. 'I thought if I could pry it loose I might use it as a weapon when they came back.'

'One against three?'

Despite their desperate situation, Tori felt a throb of satisfaction at surprising him. 'I won't go down without a fight.'

'It would be safer if you don't resist.'

Tori opened her mouth to protest but he went on.

'Three to one aren't good odds. Wait till you're alone with one of them. Someone will probably transport you elsewhere tomorrow.'

'How do you know? What did they say about me?' Her voice was harsh with fear.

He shook his head, then winced. The soft whisper that followed might have been in a language she didn't know, but she knew a curse when she heard one.

'I didn't hear them mention you,' he said finally. 'But their leader arrives tomorrow. They're expecting payment for their efforts then. They'll leave us be until he arrives.'

Tori sagged, her knees giving way suddenly. She stumbled to the wall, propping herself against it. For hours she'd been on tenterhooks, expecting at any moment—

'Are you okay?' He moved closer before stopping, as if recalling her earlier recoil.

She nodded. When she opened her mouth to reply a jagged, out-of-control laugh escaped. She clapped a hand to her lips, hating the hot tears behind her eyes and the sensation that she was on the verge of collapse.

It was ridiculous to feel relief, hearing she was safe for tonight. She was still in terrible danger. Even so, her exhausted body reacted to the news by slumping abruptly.

Firm hands caught her upper arms she sank, taking her weight and easing her descent to the floor.

His hands were big and hard, yet surprisingly gentle. Tori heard the clank of metal as he withdrew, hunkering before her.

'Sorry.' The word wobbled and she tried again. 'I just…' She looked up into dark eyes. 'What else did they say? What are they going to do with us?'

Did she imagine that his expression turned blank? In this light it was impossible to tell.

'Nothing about you.' He paused, then continued slowly. 'I have no proof, but I suspect they'll take you over the border.'

Like a smuggled commodity? Tori bit her bottom lip. She'd heard stories of the illegal slave trade, particularly in women. Nausea rose as she contemplated where she might end up.

'If that's so there might be a chance to escape. Maybe some of them will stay here.' Tori knew she was grasping at straws but it was better than giving up hope.

'I can guarantee it.' His tone grabbed her attention.

'Why? What else did you hear?'

He shrugged those wide shoulders and sank cross-legged before her. Despite the heavy chain and his injuries he looked at ease. Strange how his air of confidence reassured her.

'Their leader is my enemy. I think it fair to assume he'll be more focused on me than you.' There was a note in that deep voice that sounded almost like wry humour. Grim lines bracketed his mouth.

Suddenly Tori remembered the gesture one of their captors had made as he'd chained this man to the wall. One man had asked a question and another had laughed, a sound that had sent a chill skittering down her backbone. He'd said something sharp and dragged his finger across his throat in a gesture that crossed all languages. Death.

They were going to kill this man.

She should warn him.

Except even as she thought it she realised he knew. Tori read it in that stern face, a chiaroscuro masterpiece of male strength, and knew he wouldn't surrender to fate. Not with that pugnacious set to his jaw.

Instinctively she reached out, her hand fleetingly touching his, feeling living warmth flow into her chilled fingers. 'What can we do?'

For long seconds he surveyed her. Then gave another infinitesimal shrug. 'Check for a way out.'

'I've done that. It's *all* I've done for the last five hours or so.' That and try not to panic.

'I don't suppose you've got a hairpin?'

'For picking the lock on your handcuff?' Tori shook her head. 'I don't need hairpins with a ponytail.'

He watched the swish of her hair around her shoulders and something unexpected zipped through her. Something other than fear and despair.

Tori stilled.

'And I unfortunately didn't think to bring bolt cutters for the chain.'

She choked down a laugh. It was only mildly amusing, but in her emotional state any humour was a welcome break from constant fear.

'The windows are too small even for you.' He paused. 'The roof?'

He rose in a single fluid motion that revealed enviable core strength and left Tori gawping. A short time ago he'd been unconscious.

'Come.' He extended his hand.

She didn't know if it was the command in his tone or not, but a second later her hand was in his and he was drawing her up. They stood so close that she identified the tang of cinnamon and male, and the comforting smell of horse, before he stepped away, surveying the roof.

'Here.' He turned and beckoned.

'What do you have in mind?'

'Hands on my shoulders. I'll lift you so you can check for a way out.'

'But *you* can't get out.' Her gaze dropped to the manacle on his wrist.

'That's no reason for you not to try.'

That voice, as smooth and rich as her favourite coffee, warmed her as his gaze captured hers. Tori's racing thoughts stilled. She felt a moment of communion, as if this stranger understood the guilt that made her protest even as the idea of escape made her thrill with excitement.

'What's your name?'

The question made her pause. What would it be like to hear him ask that in different circumstances? There was something about this man...the resonance of his deep voice, his inner strength in the face of adversity, his sureness...that drew her.

Her heart beat hard against her ribs.

'Tori. And you?'

'You may call me Ash.'

Before she could wonder at his phrasing, he continued.

'If you can get onto the roof and away, there's a chance you can raise the alert before daybreak.'

He didn't have to spell out what would happen when day came. That captor's slicing gesture was vivid in her mind.

'But I don't know where I am. Or where to go.'

Long fingers folded around her hand, steadying her. 'You don't have to know. Get away from the hut and the campfire. Stay low. When you're a safe distance out, circle the camp. You'll eventually come across the trail where you entered. Keep out of sight and follow the trail.'

'And hope to find the road or a village?'

'You have a better idea?'

Tori shook her head. It was their best chance. Possibly Ash's *only* chance.

'Let's do this.' She planted her palms on his shoulders, then sucked in a breath as he bent, wrapped his big hands around her and lifted.

It was probably only fifteen minutes before they admitted defeat. To Ashraf it felt like hours.

Frustrating hours, with that cursed chain curtailing his movements. They had only been able to explore one end of the roof and it was disappointingly sturdy.

The slashing pain across his ribs had become a sear of agony. His head pounded. Stiff muscles ached from boosting his companion high, then holding her up while she strained and twisted, trying to find a weakness in the roof structure she could exploit.

Physical exertion compounded with frustration at his helplessness. But it was another sort of torture, holding Tori.

Trying to ignore her rounded breasts and buttocks. Standing solid, holding her high, his face pressed to her soft belly as she heaved and twisted, trying to force her way through the roof. Feeling the narrowness of her waist, inhaling her female essence, fresh and inviting, despite the overlay of dust and fear.

Beneath the loose trousers and long-sleeved shirt she was all woman. Firmly toned, supple and fragrantly feminine.

By the time he lowered her for the last time and sagged against the wall his body shook all over. From reaction to his wounds. From fury at himself for allowing Qadri to get the better of him.

And from arousal. Flagrant and flaming hot.

Ashraf told himself it was the adrenaline high—a response to life-or-death danger. Naturally his reactions were heightened. His need to fight his way free. His primal urge was to defy death in the same way generations had done since the dawn of time, by losing himself in the comfort of a warm, willing woman. Spilling his seed in the hope of ensuring survival, if not for himself, then for the next generation.

'Are you all right?'

She was so close her breath was a puff of warm air against his face.

'I *knew* it was too much with your wounds. We should have stopped earlier. Are you bleeding again?'

A gentle hand touched his chest just above his wound.

'Don't!' Ashraf grabbed her hand, flattening it against his chest. His eyes snapped wide and he found her staring up at him, clearly concerned. This close, he saw her eyes were pale. Blue? Grey? Maybe amber?

Realisation slammed into him.

She feels it too.

The tug of need. The connection between two people trapped and desperate. The powerful urge to find comfort in the face of impending death. For, even if she wasn't being executed in the morning, Tori's fate was dark.

'Don't fuss. I'm fine.' He pulled her palm away from his body. Yet he couldn't bring himself to relinquish her hand.

Because her touch brought unexpected comfort?

He was furious with himself for getting captured. Frustrated that, after all that had happened, maybe his life would end tomorrow and his father would have been right. The old man had said he'd never amount to anything. If Ashraf died within the first six months of his reign, with none of his changes cemented in place...

He released Tori and turned from her searching stare. 'I'm not fussing.'

She drew herself up so her head topped his chin. Her little sound of frustration reminded him of his favourite falcon, fluffing up her feathers in huffy disapproval when he didn't immediately release her for flight.

'I apologise.' He paused, surprised as the unfamiliar words escaped. 'I'm not bleeding again.' Hopefully. 'It was kind of you to be concerned.'

'Kind?' She choked on the word and it hit Ashraf that she was fighting back tears.

For him? No, she couldn't know that he faced death tomorrow. It was a reaction to her kidnap. She'd been courageous—more courageous than most men he knew—projecting a calm façade, persevering in trying to find a way out when many would have given up.

'Thoughtful,' he amended.

She shook her head and silvery hair flared out from her ponytail. Ashraf's hands curled tight. He knew an urgent desire to see that shimmering hair loose, so he could tunnel his fingers through it.

Temptation was a cruel thing. He couldn't take what he wanted. Or ask for it. Not from this proud woman who still fought panic.

'You'd better get some rest,' he murmured, his voice gruff as he ruthlessly harnessed his baser, selfish instincts. 'That's what I intend to do.'

Ashraf lowered himself to the floor. He felt every muscle, every movement. His wrist had rubbed raw against the manacle and there seemed little hope of escape.

Yet despite the pain he felt a sense of exultation. He was still alive. He had no intention of meekly submitting to execution for Qadri's pleasure.

Ashraf had spent his life fighting for his place, proving himself, ignoring the jibes. Showing his father that his disdain meant nothing. Thumbing his nose at him by building a public profile as a pleasure-seeking playboy, delighting in scandals that he knew would rock the old man.

Now he was back in Za'daq and everything had changed. Especially given his brother's recent sacrifice. Ashraf's belly contracted at the thought of Karim.

'I'd feel better if you'd let me examine your wounds.'

Tori knelt beside him. So close he barely had to move to touch her face, her rounded breast. Too close for a man so severely tempted.

'There's nothing you can do in this light. Unless you have a torch and a first aid kit hidden somewhere?'

She pursed her lips and looked away, that silvery mane sliding over one shoulder.

Instantly he regretted his harsh response. He felt ashamed. It wasn't concern for Karim that had made him snap, but his visceral sexual response to her. He wanted things he shouldn't.

'I'm sorry.' It was the second time he'd apologised. 'That was uncalled-for. You're right, there's some pain, but it's not as bad as it looks.' What were bruises and cuts in comparison to what tomorrow held for him? 'But there's something you *could* do.'

'What's that?'

'Rest. We need to conserve our strength.' He stretched out, stifling a groan as abused muscles throbbed.

After a long silence she finally followed his example, lying down nearby.

Ashraf didn't sleep. Instead he focused on tomorrow, wondering if his security detail would find him before it was too late. Wondering if Basim was alive.

Finally a tiny sound caught his attention. Were Tori's teeth chattering? The desert night had turned chill.

'Come here, Tori. We'll be warmer together.'

She lifted her head. 'But your injuries…'

He reached out his untethered arm. 'Snuggle against this side.'

When she did Ashraf bit his tongue against a sigh of satisfaction.

'Put your head on my shoulder.' She complied and he felt the gentle whisper of her breath through his torn shirt. Soft curves cushioned his side, silky strands of hair tickled his neck and her hand rested warm at his waist.

Ashraf lifted his hand to stroke her hair. It was silken. Like the softest cushions in the royal harem, spun in the days when the Sheikhs of Za'daq had had a bevy of concubines devoted to their pleasure.

Pressed against him from shoulder to knee, she felt…

His breath clogged in his lungs and a tremor started low in his body, vibrating out.

'Am I too heavy?'

She shifted as if to move away and Ashraf rolled a little towards her, capturing her knee between his.

'Just relax. You're not hurting me.'

It wasn't strictly true. He was definitely in pain. But the ache of his wounds and the indignity of the chain were eclipsed by another sort of pain. The taut stretch of a body fighting luscious temptation.

Ashraf's mouth stretched in a mirthless smile. He'd spent years giving in to temptation. He wished he had more experience at resisting it. Perhaps that was why the tension he felt was so acute, the tug of war between honour and desire so fierce.

But honour won.

Finally he felt her breathing slow. She shifted, shimmying her hips as if to get more comfortable, and the friction was exquisite torture. But it was a torture he willingly bore.

Till she moved her arm and her hand accidentally brushed the evidence of his arousal straining against his trousers.

She froze.

Everything inside him stilled.

Ashraf swore they both stopped breathing.

Then his blood pumped again—harder, more urgent. His groin tightened. He had to force himself not to tilt his pelvis, seeking the feel of her palm against him.

'It's okay. You're safe with me, Tori.' Could she tell he spoke through gritted teeth? 'Nothing's going to happen.'

Silence. He waited for her to scurry away.

Then he knew he was hearing things when she said, 'Maybe I don't want to be safe with you.'

CHAPTER TWO

TORI HEARD THE words spill out and then Ash's swift intake of breath. But she refused to play coy. Not when this might be her last night alive.

All afternoon she'd fought not to imagine what awaited her at the mercy of her kidnappers. Pain. Forced sex. Slavery.

A few hours ago she'd have said experiencing desire in her current situation was impossible. But that was before Ash. Before they worked together. Before his matter-of-fact courage bolstered her own flagging determination to be strong. Before the touch of his hand and his understanding made her feel connected to him. Before the undeniable flare of arousal ignited in her belly and saturated her skin till she burned up with it.

She knew their excruciatingly intense circumstances created the connection. Yet it wasn't quite so simple. There was something about this man that spoke to her at a primal, instinctive level. Tori knew with a resolute certainty that defied explanation that this was more than a simple response to danger.

She'd never known such a potent link. As if they'd weathered a lifetime's emotions in a couple of hours.

Never felt such an urgent need for a man.

Never felt so reckless or so absolutely sure of what she wanted.

'Tori?'

His voice was deep and gravelly, his smooth tone banished by shock. Or, she hoped, by matching desire.

She moved her hand tentatively across his flat abdomen, resisting the urge to slip it lower and explore him more intimately. Iron-hard muscles clenched at her touch and a tremor racked his big body.

Tori's heart clenched in sympathy. He was so vibrantly, emphatically alive. She couldn't bear the thought that tomorrow—

Long fingers brushed the hair back from her face, the gesture achingly tender. Then, to her horror, he stroked his thumb across her cheek and smeared the hot track of a tear she hadn't even felt fall.

'Ah, *habibti.*'

She heard the clink of metal as he wrapped his arms around her and pulled her up against him. Soft words fell into her ears as his lips moved against her eyelids, cheeks and hair. The ribbon of words was lilting and beautiful, like the unexpected sound of a spring, bubbling up clear and life-giving in a desert.

Greedily Tori drank in the sound as she absorbed his tender caresses. Blindly she tilted her head, seeking his lips, letting her leg fall across his thighs as she sought purchase to climb up his tall body.

'You have my word, Tori. If there's a way to save—'

Opening her eyes, she pressed her hand to his lips. 'Don't.'

She breathed deep, feeling her breasts push against him. Was she too heavy? But when she made to pull back the warm steel of his embrace held her.

'Don't talk about tomorrow. Please. I only want to think about tonight.'

She was so close that even in the gloom she saw the shift of muscles as he clenched his jaw. His face was strongly made, with bold lines against which the sensuous curve of his lips seemed shockingly desirable. Through the blood and dust she thought she imagined laughter lines near his eyes, but the grooves around his mouth spoke of weighty concerns.

The man's injured. He's likely to die tomorrow. Despite that, he's done his best to stop you falling apart. Of course he has more on his mind than gratifying your selfish desires.

Tori's heart contracted. He might be aroused, but that was a simple physical response to proximity and, perhaps, to danger. It didn't mean he wanted her. Perhaps he had a woman. A wife, even.

Choking back an exclamation of self-loathing, she pulled back, determined to put distance between them.

But his arms stopped her. She wriggled, trying to escape, but couldn't find purchase to resist his strength—not without elbowing his injured side.

'Let me go,' she whispered. 'I need to—'

'I know what you need, *habibti*. I need it too. So very badly.'

His voice ground low through her body, awakening those few dormant female nerve centres not already attuned to his closeness.

Tori felt herself quicken and soften, warmth spreading in a wave of anticipation for his big, hard body. Her legs splayed around his, her pelvis pressed needily against his hipbone.

Flame scorched her cheeks as one large hand slid

down to cup her bottom and pull her closer. Thoughts splintered at the dazzle of carnal pleasure erupting through her.

'I...'

She fought to find a coherent chain of thought when her body was already immersed in an intimate conversation with his. What did she want to say? The important thing?

He tilted her chin so she looked into hooded eyes. 'Talk to me, Tori. Are you certain you want this?'

She wanted it, *him*, so badly she shook with the force of her desire.

'Are you married?' The words sounded strange, in a breathless voice she hardly recognised, but now the thought had entered her head she couldn't ignore it. 'Is there anyone—?'

'No one.' His tone was grave. 'And you?'

Tori shook her head.

She felt his chest rise beneath her on a sighing breath.

Even so, what had seemed so natural, so easy, moments before, now felt difficult. She felt gauche, unsure how to proceed. Till his mouth curved slowly into a smile that stole her breath and set her heart fluttering up in her throat.

She'd had an impression of Ash as strong, ultra-masculine and handsome in a severe way. But when he bestowed that smile on her Tori discovered he was far, far more. Attractive didn't cover it. Sexy was closer. Her befuddled brain grappled for a second to find a word that did him justice. Then she gave up and simply *felt*.

His hand rose to the back of her head, pulling her closer. She went eagerly, sinking into a kiss that was devastating for all its gentle persuasiveness. Fire sizzled and sparked from her toes to her ears. From her lips to her breasts and her womb.

Her mouth softened on his, opening automatically around his tongue. She didn't even try to prevent the mew of delight as he delved deeper, inviting her to let go on the wave of wellbeing that swept her up.

The kiss went on and on, deliberate and slow, stoking the blaze between them. Till his hand cupped her breast and Tori seized up. Not in rejection, but because the sensation of that hard hand so gentle on her was exquisite.

She pulled her head back, sucking in a dizzying draught of air, meeting eyes that gleamed like obsidian in the shadowy light.

His hand froze. Clearly he'd misinterpreted her withdrawal.

Once more Tori felt a surge of respect for this man who even now let scruples override potent need.

In another place, another time, she'd want to discover everything she could about him. But they had so little time. The thought brought a desperate sob to her throat. She swallowed it and pressed his hand to her breast, revelling in the delicious sensations.

She leaned down so her lips grazed his ear. 'I want you, Ash. But I'm afraid of hurting you.' He'd stopped bleeding, but she didn't want to reopen his wounds.

She felt a rumbling beneath her that, remarkably, she identified as laughter. 'Let me worry about that.'

While she was still catching her breath he rolled her onto her back, only to freeze mid-movement. It took her a second to realise his arm was stretched out behind him, caught by the chain.

The reminder of their dire circumstances should have splintered the brief comfort of the moment. Except Ash sounded merely rueful as he murmured, 'Not my smoothest move.'

His humour made this once more about *them*, not what lay beyond these walls, and Tori bit down a smile as together they shuffled awkwardly across the floor till Ash had the freedom to move both arms.

'Better,' he whispered, gathering her close. 'Much better.'

Broad shoulders blocked out the moonlight as he bent and kissed her hard on the lips. Then, as everything in her clamoured for more, he pulled back, propping himself on his good arm as he fumbled for the zip of her trousers.

'Let me. It will be quicker.' Excitement fizzed in her blood.

When he moved back to deal with his own trousers Tori stripped off her boots, trousers and knickers. She'd never had a one-night stand but she felt no embarrassment, just an urgency that grew with every passing moment.

'Leave your shirt.' Ash's hand on her shoulder pushed her gently down onto her back. 'It will protect you from the floor.'

His own shirt hung open to reveal a wide expanse of muscled chest. Her hungry gaze began to rove him, only to stop at the dark line across a couple of ribs. Her stomach clenched.

Suddenly it wasn't sex on her mind but the fate that awaited Ash tomorrow. The thought of what they'd do to him and what they might do to her—

'Changed your mind?'

His voice held no inflection other than curiosity—as if he had no qualms about stopping. Yet even in the gloom there was no mistaking the tension in his tall frame or the sight of his arousal straining towards her.

He wanted this, needed it, as much as she.

The sight of him made her wet between the legs, her muscles tightening in anticipation. Tori drew a shuddery breath, shoving away all thoughts of tomorrow.

Live for the moment had never held such profound meaning.

'Wouldn't it be safer if I was on top? With your injuries?'

His chuckle was liquid chocolate, or perhaps a shot of malt whisky, heating her blood. 'Probably. Call me a traditionalist, but I want to lie between your beautiful thighs and take us both to Paradise.'

His words ratcheted her level of arousal from fierce to ballistic. As did the nimble way he flicked open her shirt buttons, then made short work of her front-opening bra, pulling it wide to survey her in silence.

Tori's heart battered her ribs as she felt the cold night air drift across her puckering nipples and waited for his next move. Then he smiled. Another of those charismatic smiles that drove a spike of sharp emotion straight through her rib cage and stopped her breath.

When he spoke again it was in a language she didn't understand. A fluid ripple of sound that wrapped itself around her, caressing her as effectively as those callused hands stroking her breasts, waist and hips. Drawing her into a world of seductive urgency.

Then Ash lowered himself over her and she almost cried out at how right it felt. Strong, hair-roughened thighs between hers. The weight of him heavy against her. The jut of his hipbones. Broad shoulders above her and heat…heat everywhere.

Tori drew her knees up above his hips and heard a grunt of masculine pleasure. Then long fingers slid low, past her abdomen, down to her hot, slick, swollen centre. She jolted as a shock of pleasure raced through her. His fingers moved again, circling and teasing.

Her hand on his wrist stopped him. 'No. Don't. I just want *you*.'

She was strung so tight, on an unbearable edge of arousal, that she feared one more touch might fling her into rapture. But she needed something more profound than the touch of his hand. She craved the ultimate connection, the intimacy of their two bodies linked as one.

Tori sighed her relief when he nodded. Even so Ash took his time, surveying her face as if memorising it. Tori *felt* his gaze cross her cheeks, lips and forehead. And when his hand brushed the hair back from her face it was a gesture that spoke of tenderness and restraint, for she felt the tiniest tremor in those long fingers.

'Your hair is like silk,' he murmured.

Tori wanted to say something profound, to offer this strong, gentle man something to match the gift of his tenderness. But there were no easy words.

Instead she lifted her own hand, cupping the stubble-roughened jaw, hard and warm. She felt his slow pounding pulse, then skimmed her hand higher into dark hair that felt thick yet soft. His eyes closed as she massaged the uninjured side of his scalp.

He positioned himself against her. Instinctively she lifted her pelvis, feeling that velvet weight nudge her. Tori held her breath as he pushed, long and slow and further, surely, than any previous possession. Her eyes widened and his grew more heavy-lidded as they held their breaths at the perfection of their joining. The moment went on and on till finally Ash was lodged deep within, vital and impossibly, lavishly male.

A quiver ran through Tori, starting at the muscles surrounding him and spreading till she trembled all over. A matching shiver rippled across his wide shoulders and muscled arms.

Then he withdrew, and the movement was so exquisitely arousing that Tori had to bite her lip to stop from crying out. Ash's lips pulled back in a grimace that looked like pain, but she knew it was a sign of pleasure and his battle for control.

The sight of him fighting for restraint and the generous pleasure of his returning thrust sent Tori spiralling over the edge.

'Please.' Her hands dug into his shoulders as she struggled to keep her voice to a whisper. 'I need you now.'

Ash's mouth covered hers, blotting out the scream rising within. Strong arms held her close as he abandoned restraint and pounded fast, hard and satisfying, filling her so that it seemed there was no longer Tori and Ash but only one being, straining after pleasure. Rapture exploded in a shuddering conflagration so powerful that the very air vibrated with it.

Together they rocked and shuddered. She was overwhelmed by sensations so intense they defied description. Except that at their heart was a delight so profound Tori half expected to die from it.

The world shook. Senses swam. Blood roared in her ears loud as a helicopter coming in to land. And through it all they stayed locked together, mouths and bodies fused.

Finally, when sanity began to creep back in, Ash rolled onto his side and then his back, taking Tori with him.

Aftershocks ripped through her as overloaded pleasure receptors reacted again and again.

A rough gasp of pain reminded her of Ash's wounds. Instantly she tried to shift from his grasp. He didn't need her weight on his injuries.

'Stay.' His voice was hoarse, a rough wisp of sound that Tori found it impossible to resist.

She kissed him open-mouthed in the hot, male-scented curve where his shoulder met his neck. He shivered, hauling her closer.

Never had Tori felt this profound oneness. It was shared physical pleasure but surely something more. Something inexplicable that had swept them up and cradled them together.

Tori gave in to the protective urge to spread her arms as wide as she could around his brawny shoulders. She rested her head on his chest, absorbing the reassuring heavy thud of his heartbeat. She'd wait till she caught her breath. Then she'd try to define the change she sensed with every cell yet couldn't name.

It was her last cogent thought for hours.

'Tori.'

The luscious deep voice was warm and seductive in her ear. Ash's hands moved over her body and she stretched sinuously, arching to meet them.

She frowned, for he wasn't caressing her, he was—

'It's time to wake up.' His hands were deftly doing up her shirt buttons, right to the collar.

'Ash?' She opened her eyes to discover pale light filtering through the small windows.

He was dressed, she realised, his torn shirt buttoned and tucked into dusty trousers. Then she recalled him insisting in the night that they dress again. For warmth, he'd said.

Now she felt a chill that was only partly due to the temperature. Grey dawn light revealed a clearer view of Ash than she'd had so far. His features were starkly sculpted and compelling. His face would turn any woman's head. But now she saw clearly the blood caked in his hair. His torn clothes were liberally marked with dark stains and the chain securing him looked brutally heavy.

Tori's stomach turned as dread reality hit her full-force. Nausea rose. Her pulse accelerated to a panicky rhythm. Impossibly, in Ash's arms the peril they were in had been pushed to the back of her mind. Now re-alisation slammed into her.

She clutched his hands and he paused. His eyes met hers and something passed between them. Then Ash took hold of her hands. In this light she still couldn't make out the colour of his eyes, yet the warmth she read in them counteracted the chill crackling across her bones.

Slowly, as if he had all the time in the world, he raised her left hand and kissed her palm, his warm lips soft on her flesh. He repeated the gesture with her other hand, sending a squiggle of heat from her palms to her breasts and lower, arrowing to her core.

He murmured something against her palm that she couldn't catch. But his eyes as they met hers glowed with a message that made her chest clamp.

'Thank you, *habibti*.' He inclined his head, sketching a quick, graceful movement with his hand that spoke of respect and admiration. 'You did me great honour last night. Your gift is one I'll carry with me.'

Tori was about to respond when Ash's expression changed. His head whipped towards the door, his features intent, as if he heard something she couldn't.

'Quickly.' He grabbed her boots and shoved her feet into them.

'What is it?'

But she guessed the cause of his urgency. Someone was coming.

The thought of their captors made her fingers shake, and she watched Ash push her hands aside to do up the laces with swift efficiency.

'Remember what I said.' His voice was urgent and low. 'Don't fight back till you're alone with one of them. You'll stand a better chance.'

Tori looked into that stern, handsome face and nodded. She swallowed hard. 'You—?'

'I'll be fine. Now the sun's rising the search party will find it easier to locate the camp.'

Neither admitted that the search party might be too late for him.

His hands tightened on hers as they heard voices outside. Leaning in, he whispered, 'When you escape—' *when*, not *if*… Tori's heart leapt with hope '—keep low and—'

His words were cut off by the door banging open to rattle against the wall. Tori blinked against the light, realising belatedly that Ash no longer held her hands but was on his feet, facing the three men who had entered.

What came next was the stuff of nightmares. Brutal, pawing hands and leering faces. A slap that made her head ring as she struggled to free herself. But far worse was the sight of Ash, pulling one of the men off her and then being set upon by two of them. Hampered by the chain, he was eventually overwhelmed by vicious blows to his injured head and ribs.

The last she saw of him he'd crumpled to his knees and then pitched sideways, a scarlet bloom spilling from his wounds across the dirt floor.

The rusty tang of fresh blood was sharp in Tori's nostrils as she was shoved, stumbling, into the chill morning.

CHAPTER THREE

TORI STARED AT the data before her, wishing she could blame her lack of concentration on a post-lunch slump. Stretching, she leaned back in her chair and took in the view of Perth's Swan River, sparkling in the sunlight.

It had been tough, moving from Sydney to Western Australia. She'd had to find a new home, start a new job, create a new life, all on top of the trauma that still haunted her.

If her father had been at all supportive she'd have settled in Sydney. Family was supposed to be there for you during difficult times, after all.

Tori shuddered, remembering the last time she and her father had spoken. It was pointless wishing for the impossible—like a caring father—but his icy disapproval on top of recent events had made Tori miss her mother more than ever. She'd been warm, practical and supportive. Tori could have done with the unconditional love that had died years before, with her mother.

Yet it wasn't any of those things distracting her now. Or even last night's broken sleep. She was used now to perennial tiredness.

It was the date. Fifteen months to the day since she'd been kidnapped in Za'daq.

She'd been about to leave Assara, her geological survey complete and her companions already gone. She'd spent her final afternoon investigating an outcrop that hadn't been in her survey zone but had looked promising.

Until she'd found herself surrounded by armed men.

Fifteen months since she'd last seen Ash.

Fifteen months since the sharp rattle of gunfire had echoed across the arid landscape, raising the hairs on her arms and neck and devastating her.

She'd never forget that sound.

Or the gloating chuckle of the leader of the small party that had left the bandit camp to make its way across the foothills.

He was the one Ash had knocked aside after the man had grabbed her, his hands insinuating themselves under her shirt. When gunfire had sounded from the camp the man had leered, slicing his hand across his throat in a violent gesture. He'd spat out words she hadn't understood but his meaning had been clear. Ash was dead.

Even now the nightmare reality was almost too much to take in.

The fruit smoothie she'd had for lunch curdled in Tori's stomach and she swallowed hard, trying to keep it down.

Traumatic memories were normal, her counsellor said. And, what with having been up half the night, it was no surprise that Tori was susceptible today to distressing flashes of memory.

They'd pass. They always did.

Meanwhile she had a report to sort out.

Breathing deep, she turned back to her computer.

She was frowning over an anomaly when a waft of pungent aftershave reached her.

'Head down, Victoria? Good to see you making the most of the time you're actually in the office.'

Tori repressed a sigh. It *would* be Steve Bates—leader of the other team on this floor. He always carped about her part-time hours, implying that she took advantage of the company instead of actually working harder than some of her full-time colleagues. And that never stopped him staring at her as if he could see through her clothes.

She needed to tackle him about his attitude. But not today, when she felt so low. Besides, she'd survived far worse than Steve could dish out.

The thought steadied her.

Tori swung around in her chair to meet his stare. Naturally it wasn't her face he was looking at. She sat straighter and his eyes lifted.

'This new survey data is intriguing. Is that why you're here? I'll have the report ready by—'

He stopped her with a dismissive wave. 'I'm not here for that.' He paused, his X-ray stare focused on her face, his gaze sharply assessing. 'You're full of surprises, aren't you?'

Tori frowned. 'Sorry?'

Steve smiled, but instead of putting her at ease his calculating expression made disquiet flicker.

'I had no idea you had such…connections. No wonder the bosses were eager to snap you up. But then it's always who you know, isn't it? Not how good your work is.'

'Now, look here!' She shot to her feet, fury rising. She had no patience for people who thought she'd got where she was through her father's influence. 'I won this job on merit. Simple as that.'

The idea of her father interfering on her behalf wasn't

just wrong, it was risible. Despite what he said in public, Jack Nilsson didn't approve of her career. As for exerting himself on her behalf... Not unless it would win him positive publicity.

'If you say so.' Steve raised his hands but his knowing smirk lingered. 'Don't be so touchy and emotional.'

Tori raised one eyebrow at the typical putdown. When she spoke again she used the clear, carrying tones she'd learned when her father had insisted she take up debating at school. 'Was there a work matter you wanted to discuss? Or did you just interrupt me to shoot the breeze?'

Steve slanted a glance towards the open-plan office behind him. His expression grew ugly. 'You're wanted in the boardroom.' His tone was as hard as the diamonds the company mined. 'Immediately.'

He turned on his heel and disappeared, leaving Tori relieved and confused. She hated Steve's snarky sexism. He deserved far more than the mild rebuke she'd given him. But she had no idea who wanted to see her and why. She knew where the boardroom was, but she wasn't significant enough in the company to be invited to meetings there.

She tried to remember if she'd heard anything about an executive meeting today but nothing registered.

Tori smoothed her hair then reached for her phone, her tablet and the not yet finished survey report. Taking a deep breath, she marched across the office, feeling curious glances as she pushed the lift button for the executive level.

Minutes later she stepped into the rarefied atmosphere of extreme wealth. The company was one of the most successful of its type and the executive suite was all plush carpet, expensive artworks and bespoke wood panelling. The views up here were dizzyingly spectacular.

Tori was staring about her when a young man in a pinstriped suit approached.

'Ms Nilsson?'

His manner was friendly, but there was no mistaking his curiosity. She resisted the urge to check her hair or straighten her collar. She'd learned never to fidget in public. Her father hated it because it spoiled the perfect press shot.

'Yes. I understand I'm wanted in the boardroom?' She let her voice rise at the end of the sentence, hinting at a question. But he didn't offer an explanation.

'That's right. This way, please.'

He led the way past a beautifully appointed lounge with panoramic windows. As they approached a set of double doors Tori noticed a man in a dark suit nearby. His feet were planted wide and his hands clasped.

A bodyguard. She'd seen enough of them to recognise the demeanour.

This one met her eyes calmly, no doubt sizing her up. He looked sturdy and, despite his impassive expression, intimidating.

Tori gripped her belongings tighter. Unusual that one of the company's executives should bring a bodyguard into the building. Then she remembered Steve's snide challenge. *'It's always who you know.'*

Which meant it was her father in the boardroom. Though why he'd brought a bodyguard... And why he'd chosen to meet her at work... He hadn't mentioned coming to Western Australia and he never made paternal visits.

'Here you are, Ms Nilsson.' Her guide pushed open one of the doors.

She stepped in to find the room empty. There was no meeting. The long polished table was bare.

Tori blinked and hesitated. She was about to go out again and ask what was going on when a shadow at the far end of the room detached itself from the wall.

A man. A tall man, spine straight and shoulders wide. He was silhouetted against a wall of glass. For an instant all she had was an impression of strength and the loose-limbed saunter of an athlete as he approached. She didn't recognise the walk, but there was something familiar about him.

Tori's skin tightened as premonition swept through her. A split-second certainty that she knew him.

She opened her mouth to say hello, but then he drew close enough that she could make out his features instead of just the shape of his head.

Tori heard a hissed breath. Her hands slackened. Something hard grazed her shin as it dropped with a thud onto the carpeted floor. But her gaze was glued to the man who had stopped just an arm's length away.

Bronzed skin pulled tight over a bone structure that would have made Michelangelo weep. A sensual mouth set above a determined jaw. Eyes that even from here looked black rather than dark brown. Black eyebrows. A forceful nose that transformed his face from an ideal of masculine beauty to one of power. Black hair that Tori knew was soft to the touch.

Her nerveless hands twitched as memory flooded through her. Of channelling her fingers through hair so soft and thick it felt like a pelt. Of being careful to avoid the clotted blood of his head injury.

The twitch in her hands became a tremor. A shudder thundered through her as her heart crashed into her ribs.

Heat suffused her as she met gleaming eyes. Then a wash of icy cold as other memories battered her brain.

Kidnappers. Gunfire.

Her eyes prickled and she blinked rapidly. Tears came easily now—another thing her counsellor said was normal. Yet instinctively Tori tried to dam them.

She swayed. The floor seemed to ripple and the walls appeared to close around the man watching her so intently. Tori grabbed the back of a leather conference chair for support, fingers clawing.

There was no scarring on his face. Nothing to indicate he'd ever been brutalised or shot at. He wore a dark grey suit tailored by an expert. It rivalled anything in her father's expensive wardrobe, and on this man's rangy, powerful frame looked spectacular. A white shirt complemented his burnished skin and a perfectly knotted silk tie completed the image of urbane sophistication.

It couldn't be. It was impossible. And yet…

'I thought you were dead.'

It didn't sound like her voice, so husky and uneven. Yet he understood. His eyes widened and something passed across his face.

'Ah, that explains a lot.'

That voice! That deep, rich voice. She'd only heard him whisper before. They'd both kept their voices low so as not to attract the guards' attention. His whispers had threaded through her dreams for over a year. How often had she woken from a nightmare or the occasional erotic dream with the sound of his voice in her head?

'It *is* you?'

Tori wanted to touch him, to check for herself he was

no mirage. But her limbs felt like blocks of basalt. All
she could do was stand and stare.

'It's me, Tori.'

Ashraf stared down into her oval face and felt a wave
of emotion tumble through him.

He'd searched for her so long, against impossible
odds, when even the best investigators had advised him
to give up. He recalled the moment he'd received news
that she was alive. Alive and safe. Relief had been so
intense, so powerful, that for a moment he'd found it
difficult to breathe.

He'd been fully prepared for this meeting, and still
reality was nothing like his expectation.

Seeing Tori in the flesh unsettled him profoundly.

Maybe it was her eyes. He'd wondered about their
colour. Now he knew. Soft blue. The colour of the dainty
yet hardy forget-me-nots that grew in Za'daq's moun-
tain valleys. Her gaze held his and he felt the bite of
need, of hunger, of regret and a hundred emotions he
wasn't in the habit of feeling. Those lovely eyes shone
over-bright and her lip quivered.

Deep inside something responded with an intensity
that rocked him back on his heels. As if his feelings
were engaged in a way that was totally unfamiliar.

He'd admired her in Za'daq. She'd been courageous
and strong, hiding her fears. He'd found comfort and
welcome oblivion in her lithe body.

But he hadn't expected such a visceral reaction after
all this time. He'd told himself danger had heightened
their responses.

Ashraf registered the thunder of his pulse and the
tingling in his blood that betrayed a surge of adrena-

line. He wanted to touch her. More than touch her. He wanted—

He slammed a door on such thoughts. His reason for being here was too important for distraction. Despite other unexpected urges. To comfort and assure her. To protect her as he hadn't been able to fifteen months ago.

Guilt sliced at the memory. But it was blunted by other emotions. Desire. Possessiveness, rampant and untrammelled.

Ashraf tunnelled his fists into his pockets and forced himself to stand his ground rather than close the space between them.

'You need to sit. You've had a shock.'

She blinked up, eyes round and lips open as if she couldn't get enough oxygen.

He knew the feeling. His lungs were labouring as if he were the one surprised. He hadn't expected to feel—

Ashraf leaned past her, pulling out a high-backed chair from the table, and gestured for her to sit. She did, and he saw that even in extremity there was a familiar grace about her movements. He'd thought he'd imagined that, embellished his recollections of this woman with qualities she hadn't actually possessed. He'd told himself guilt and regret had turned her in his mind into someone more remarkable than she really was.

Striving for emotional distance, he catalogued what he saw. She was the same as in the photos his investigators had sent. Yet she was *more*.

Regular features in a face that was long rather than round. Fine lips. Even finer eyes. Eyes that watched his every move with an intensity he felt as a sizzle in his veins. Even the faint shadows of tiredness didn't mar her attractiveness. The hair he'd remembered as pale was platinum-blonde, pulled back and up in a chignon that left her face clear. But why would she hide those cheekbones? She wasn't classically beautiful, yet he defied any man not to take a second look.

Even in a plain white blouse and black trousers Tori Nilsson drew the eye.

That explained his racing pulse. That and the intimate secret they shared.

For a second his attention lingered on those breasts, quickly rising and falling against her blouse. They seemed plumper than he remembered—

'Can you sit, instead of towering over me?'

Ashraf huffed back laughter. *There* was the woman he remembered. Indomitable and practical. How lucky he'd been not to be stuck with a hysterical companion that night.

He pulled out a chair and sat knee to knee with her.

'You're really real.'

Slim fingers skimmed shakily over his cheek, down his freshly shaved jaw, and two things struck him.

First, no one these days ever touched him. He'd been busy in the last two years and it had been a long time since he'd had a lover. Plus his position meant that casual touching was out of the question.

Second, her hand shook. Perhaps he'd been unfair, confronting her like this with no warning. But he hadn't known she'd believed him dead. If he'd realised...

No, even if he'd known he'd still have wanted to see her in person.

'Yes. I'm real.'

He captured her hand, feeling the quick pulse throb at her wrist. At the same time he registered a hint of scent. Something sweet and enticing, slightly citrusy.

It transported him to that night they'd been captives together. He couldn't recall noticing it then, but at some subliminal level he must have. It both enticed and disturbed him, reminding him of how close they'd come to death, and how he'd allowed himself to weaken in this woman's arms.

He released her hand and brushed her cheek with his knuckles. Satiny skin trembled at his touch and made his blood fizz.

He'd assumed his physical response to Tori had been fuelled by danger, by the knowledge that he might die. Was this just a hangover from that night? That had to be it.

But he wasn't here for sex.

Ashraf dropped his hand and sat back.

'How did you get away? I heard gunfire. I thought—'

Tori bit her lip, hearing the wobble in her voice. Clearly she'd thought wrong—so why was she upset? Seeing Ash again was a miracle. One she'd never dared hope for. Her reaction had to be due to shock.

'You thought they'd shot me?' His eyebrows rose and then he nodded. 'I'm sure they wish they had. You heard security forces storming the camp. Qadri, the bandits' leader, had just arrived. He was killed in the raid with several of his followers. The rest are serving time for various offences—including kidnap.'

The words sounded matter-of-fact. Like a news report of some distant, almost unreal incident. But the sound of those guns had been brutal reality for Tori for too long. She strove to absorb Ash's news but couldn't prevent a tremor of reaction.

'I thought you were dead. I—' She searched his face,

even now finding it hard to believe he was there and whole. 'What are you *doing* here? It's an incredible co-incidence.'

'No coincidence, Tori. I've been looking for you.' His voice was deep and assured.

'You have?'

Ash sat straighter. 'Of course! Did you imagine I'd forget about you? That I'd leave you to the mercy of people-smugglers?'

'But it's been fifteen months!'

His dark eyes flashed. 'I'm not in the habit of forgetting my friends.'

Was that what they'd been? Friends? Allies, for sure. Lovers too. And now...?

'I regret it took so long. I'd imagined...'

He shook his head, as if his imaginings weren't important, but the grim set of his mouth told its own story. If she'd been tormented by the thought of him dead, he'd had the burden of thinking her at the mercy of men like those who'd kidnapped her.

Tori closed her hand over his fist where it rested on his thigh. 'I'm not blaming you, Ash. That wasn't a rebuke. I'm just...surprised.' Make that astounded. She'd never in her wildest dreams believed she'd see him again. 'How did you locate me?'

He shrugged. 'A team of top investigators, persistence and in the end one lucky break.'

Investigators working for fifteen months? That must have cost a fortune.

Tori's gaze skittered across that beautifully made suit. Ash wasn't ostentatiously dressed but he projected an aura of authority and wealth, like a man used to wielding power. A little like her father, except in Ash it seemed innate, less cultivated for public consumption. Her father revelled in the importance his position gave him. Ash, on the other hand, wasn't showy or obvious.

'You're a determined man.'

If there'd been an easy trail to follow he'd have found her ages ago. The fact that he'd persevered all this time spoke of a doggedness she could only admire. If she'd still been at the mercy of people-smugglers she was sure he'd have found a way to free her. The knowledge made her heart lurch.

'How did you get away? Month after month my people scoured Za'daq and the border territory for you. They found nothing.'

My people. He made it sound as if he had his own personal army.

Belatedly Tori realised she still held his hand. She forced her fingers open and sat back, folding her hands together and telling herself the throb of heat she felt had nothing to do with touching Ash.

But hearing he'd made it his quest to find her unravelled something she'd kept locked up tight since the horror of the kidnap. And looking into those dark eyes was messing with her head. She squeezed her eyes closed and drew a breath.

This was so complicated. So profoundly difficult. What on earth was she going to do?

'Tori?'

She snapped her eyes open. 'Sorry. I'm still a little stunned.'

The implications of Ash being here were only just seeping into her whirling brain. There was so much to consider. So many variables and, yes, worries. Her skin prickled with anxiety and it wasn't from reliving the past.

But for now she owed him her story.

'Three of us rode away from the camp. Me, the guard you knocked down and a boy—barely a teenager. When we heard the gunshots the older man was happy. He thought you were dead.' Tori snatched a fortifying breath, remembering the sour tang of fear and horror she'd felt at his gleeful triumph. 'But after the first couple of shots he said something to the boy and then headed back the way we'd come.'

'Probably realised there was too much gunfire for an execution.'

Slowly Tori nodded. She hadn't considered that. She'd thought the firing squad had been overly enthusiastic, or perhaps celebrating.

'The pair of us kept riding, but the boy wasn't happy. He began to look scared. Maybe he understood some English, because I told him what would happen to him when he was caught. I might have exaggerated...'

'Good for you!' Ash looked admiring and Tori was amazed at how good that felt.

'What did I have to lose? Besides, I was upset.'

An understatement for the raw rage and fear that had consumed her as they'd trekked through the wilderness. Hearing that gunfire and believing Ash dead had been a living nightmare. Even remembering that moment—

'Go on.'

Tori spread her hands. 'It wasn't really hard to get away. I realised later he let me escape.'

Ash nodded. 'He must have realised something had gone wrong and he'd be in trouble if he was found with you.'

'I ran away during a rest stop. The rope was a little loose and I eventually got it undone. I was terrified he'd come after me but I never saw him again.'

Tori flexed her hands, remembering the burn of dust against red raw flesh.

'Hours later I stumbled into the path of a four-wheel drive. A couple of foreigners were returning to their private yacht after a trip inland.'

Foreigners who had been sympathetic but, for reasons of their own, avoiding the authorities. She'd wondered if they were smuggling contraband.

'They were on their way to the Maldives and took me with them. Once there I made contact with the Australian authorities.'

'You crossed the border from Za'daq into Assara,' Ash said. 'We made enquiries in neighbouring countries, but using official channels it was a slow process with no leads. It was only recently that a witness came forward. A driver passing through on his way to a family wedding. Recently he returned to visit his village again and heard about the search for you. He remembered three foreigners boarding a yacht in a deserted cove.'

Tori digested that. 'And from something so vague you located me?' It was remarkable! She could barely imagine the resources, or sheer luck, required to find her.

'Eventually. Fortunately the yacht was distinctive, so it could be tracked. Your trail was easy from the Maldives, after I knew you'd escaped and where you were headed.' His mouth twisted ruefully. 'If we'd exchanged full names and addresses it would have saved time.'

Heat tickled Tori's throat. Despite their physical intimacy they'd never got past first names. It seemed strange now.

'Well, you found me. I'm glad.' She smiled up at him. Despite the complications she'd now have to face, it was wonderful to know he'd survived. 'It's good to see you alive.'

'And you, Tori.'

His look seared her and she shifted in her seat. It wasn't just relief she felt. Her emotions were complex and she found herself growing nervous all over again.

The longer she sat with him, the more she realised how little she knew about Ash, despite the way her body hummed with awareness. He seemed light-years away from the stoic man with whom she'd shared intimacies in the desert.

She couldn't imagine—

No, that was wrong. She *could* imagine all too easily the urge to be with him again. The realisation sent heat spiralling through her middle and surging up her throat to scald her cheeks.

Yet it wasn't sexual awareness stretching her nerves tight. It was apprehension. For she knew next to nothing about him. His life, hopes, expectations. How he'd react when faced with what she had to tell him.

For a craven moment she wondered if she could avoid that. It would be taking a giant step into the unknown. But it had to be done.

She moistened her lips, ready to speak, but he was too fast for her.

'So, Tori. Or should I call you Victoria?' He leaned closer, his black-as-night gaze pinioning her to the seat. 'Are you going to tell me about my son?'

CHAPTER FOUR

IF ASHRAF HAD had any doubts about the child being his, they were banished by Tori's reaction.

The flush colouring her face disappeared completely, leaving those high-cut cheeks blanched like porcelain. Her gasp filled the silent room.

His investigators had provided a photo—part of a slim dossier on Victoria Miranda Nilsson. A photo of a tiny child with dark hair and what might be dark eyes, though the shot had been taken from too far away to be sure.

Now he was sure. She'd had his baby.

Another surge of adrenaline shot into his blood, catapulting around his body. It took everything he had to sit there, holding her gaze, instead of erupting to his feet and pacing the length of the room.

But Ashraf had learned in childhood to control his impulses, even if later he'd made his name by giving in to them. No, that wasn't quite right. Even when he'd gone out of his way to provoke with scandal and headlines his actions hadn't been impulsive, even if they'd seemed so. They'd been carefully considered for maximum impact.

But now wasn't the time to think of his father and

how they'd always been on opposing sides. Now *he* was a father.

Ashraf registered awe as the reality of it sideswiped him. As he thought of this slim, self-possessed woman fruitful with his child. How had she looked, her belly rounded with his baby? Did that explain the urge he now battled to feel her pliant body against his again? Because she'd borne his child? He wished he'd been there, seeing her body change, attending the birth. So much he'd missed out on. So much she'd had to face without him.

'I was going to tell you, Ash. I was just…' She waved her hand in a vague gesture at odds with the determined tilt of her chin.

How wrong he'd been—imagining she'd deliberately withheld the news of his son.

Satisfaction eddied in his belly that his first assessment of her appeared right after all. He'd thought her practical, brave and honest. He'd admired her, wanted to believe she'd got away. Yet when finally he'd received proof that she had, doubts had filtered in. Because she hadn't informed him about the baby.

Now he knew why.

What had she gone through, having his child alone? Without, as far as he could tell, family support? She'd believed him dead. Her shock on seeing him had been no charade. Ashraf tried to imagine how she'd felt, struggling with the effects of trauma alone when she'd most needed assistance.

'You're still in shock. You thought me dead.'

'It's true! I did.' She spoke so quickly she must have read something in his expression.

'I believe you.'

'But?'

He lifted his shoulders, spreading his hands. 'In my work I sometimes appear on the television news. It seemed likely you'd see me.' That had been one of the reasons he'd feared for her—feared that she was dead or unable to contact him.

'Do you? You must have an important job.'

When he merely shrugged she laughed, the sound short, almost gruff.

'My father is a politician. Years of being force-fed a diet of politics means I avoid the TV news.'

Cynicism threaded her soft voice. A dislike of politicians or just her father?

'Especially news from Za'daq.' Another wide gesture with her hand. 'After what happened I've actively avoided reports from that part of the world.'

Now he saw it in her eyes. Not prevarication but a haunted look that spoke of pain and trauma. Her abduction had left scars.

His hand captured hers, reassuring. He was pleased to feel its warmth. She looked so pale he'd imagined her chilled. Yet when they touched there was a definite spark of fire.

'Besides,' she went on, 'new mothers have priorities other than TV current affairs programmes.'

The baby. *His* baby. That had been her priority.

Now it was his too.

Ashraf would do everything necessary to ensure his son had the sort of life he deserved.

'Tell me about him.'

She looked down at his hand enfolding hers, then away. 'He's the most important thing in my life.'

'As he will be in mine,' he vowed.

Startled eyes flashed to his. Ashraf felt the shock of contact, read the flare of…was that *fear*? Then Tori looked away. This time she slipped her hand back into her lap, curving her other hand protectively around it.

Tori looked into those gleaming eyes and her heart stuttered. Had she ever seen a man so intent?

Yes. The night she and Ash had made love, finding solace in each other's arms. Finding rapture.

For so long she'd wondered what it would be like if Ash hadn't died. If he'd been at her side through the pregnancy and birth, and later to care for Oliver. The thought was a secret refuge when the burdens she'd faced grew too heavy.

Now she discovered her fantasy was real—too real, given her response to him. And Tori had to remind herself that he wasn't the embodiment of her exhausted daydreams but a man with his own agenda.

A shuddery sigh began deep in her belly and travelled up through lungs that contracted hard, stealing her breath, making her turn away.

Ash had done that to her fifteen months ago—stolen her breath, her senses, her self-possession. Now he was doing it again, without trying.

She was in deep trouble. If she'd learned one thing about him, it was that he followed through. When he determined to do something he did it.

Now he'd staked a claim on his son.

Her son. Her precious Oliver.

Suddenly, as if she'd taken an unwary step and plunged off a precipice, Tori was out of her depth.

The working part of her brain told her she should be used to that by now. After her kidnap and escape.

After childbirth alone and unsupported by anyone except the competent, kind midwives who'd delivered her son. After relocating to the far side of the country to build a life for her darling boy free of her father.

But this time it felt different. Perhaps because what she shared with Ash was so personal. Not merely her body and her passion, but her son.

Did he expect her to give Oliver up? She knew little of Middle Eastern culture but guessed fathers might have more authority there than mothers.

Her gaze slewed back to Ash to find him watching her with a stillness that did nothing to assuage her nerves. It was the stillness of a predator.

Tori dragged in a deep breath. She was overreacting. Ash wasn't a bully. He was…

She didn't know what he was.

'You'll want to see him.'

Even saying it sent a wobble through her middle, as if she was walking a tightrope and one misstep would send her tumbling.

He inclined his head. 'Of course.'

'That's why you came.'

Now it became clear. If he'd hired investigators to find her they would have discovered she'd travelled to Western Australia accompanied by her infant son.

Tori wrapped her arms around herself.

One dark eyebrow climbed that broad forehead. 'I was searching for *you*, Tori. And when I discovered you'd given birth to a child nine months after the night we spent together…' His straight shoulders lifted in a fluid shrug. 'Of course I wanted to come myself. To hear your explanation.'

Explanation. As if she'd done something wrong—

namely deprived him of his child. Was he here to pun-
ish her for that? Perhaps by taking Oliver from her?

No, that was unfair. Nothing she'd learned about Ash
that night indicated he was anything but decent and
admirable. Besides, would she have liked him if he'd
learned about her baby and ignored the fact? If he'd
shied away from responsibility?

The nervous roiling in her stomach settled a little as
the thought penetrated. She was allowing fear to build
upon fear, when the little she knew about Ash should
have reassured her.

The Ash she'd met last year.

This man, in his hand-stitched suit with an air of as-
surance in the plush executive suite, was someone she
had yet to know.

'If I'd known you were alive I'd have told you about
Oliver.'

'Oliver...' He said it slowly, rolling the name around
his tongue as if testing it.

'Oliver Ashal Nilsson.' Fire climbed her throat and
moved higher, making her ears tingle.

'Ashal?' Both eyebrows arched this time. 'That's an
Arabic name.'

So his investigators hadn't got as far as checking
the birth certificate. For some reason that made her
feel better.

'I know. I wanted...' She dropped her gaze to her
knotted hands. 'I wanted him to have something from
you so I gave him your name—or as close to it as I
could find. I wasn't sure if Ash was your real name.'

She looked up to see Ash staring at her as if he'd
never seen her before. He swallowed and she tracked
the movement of his strong throat, finding it strangely

both arousing and endearing, as if it indicated he was affected by the revelation.

Perhaps her imagination worked overtime.

'I found Ashal in a list of baby names. It means light or radiance.'

'I know what it means.'

Ash's voice was so low Tori felt it trawl through her belly.

'It's a fine name.' He paused. 'It was very generous of you to give him a name that honoured my heritage.'

Tori spread her hands. 'It seemed apt. He's the light of my life.'

Awareness pulsed between them. Not sexual this time, but an unprecedented moment of understanding. The sort she imagined parents the world over shared when they discussed their beloved children. It reassured her as nothing else had.

'So what *is* your name? Is it Ash?'

'Ashraf.'

'Ashraf.' She said it slowly, liking the sound.

'It means most honourable or noble.' His mouth kicked up at the corner, lending his expression a fleetingly cynical cast. A second later the impression was gone. 'Ashraf ibn Kahul al Rashid.'

He watched her closely as if expecting a reaction. Something about the name tickled her memory but she couldn't place it.

When she merely nodded he went on, 'Sheikh of Za'daq.'

'Sheikh?' Weren't they just in books?

'Leader.' He paused. 'Prince. Ruler.'

Tori's mouth dried. She swallowed, then swiped her

bottom lip with her tongue. 'You're the ruler of Za'daq? Of the whole country?'

For the second time in half an hour the world tilted around her. Hands braced on the chair's cushioned armrests, she fought sudden dizziness.

Oliver's father was a *king*?

'That explains the bodyguard.'

If she'd known what waited for her in this room, would she have entered or turned tail and run?

'Basim? He's head of my close personal protection team.'

No wonder Ash—no, Ashraf—had spoken of *his people* scouring the land, searching for her. His protection team must have been beside themselves when he was abducted.

'Do many people want to kill you?' Tori's thoughts had already veered to her tiny son and his safety.

'Not any more. Za'daq is actually a peaceful, law-abiding country. But it's customary and sensible to take precautions. Besides, it's expected that a visiting head of state will bring a security detail.'

Head of state. There it was again—that horrible slam of shock to her insides, creating a whirl of anxious nausea.

'Breathe.'

Firm hands clasped hers, anchoring them to the arms of the chair. A waft of spice and heat surrounded her, tantalising.

Tori stared up into fathomless eyes that looked like pure ebony even now as Ash...Ashraf...leaned in. Eyes so like Oliver's, and yet their impact was completely different from the feelings evoked when she looked at her son.

'I'm breathing. You can let me go.'

Even so it took one, two, three rapid beats of her heart before he released her. Was she crazy to think she saw regret in his expression?

'It's hard to believe after our abduction, I know, but you could travel in that same area unharmed today.'

'You said he was your enemy?' Tori murmured. 'That man—Qadri. In Australia, even in politics, when you speak of an enemy you don't mean someone who'd have you executed at dawn.' Even if the backstabbing and political manoeuvring in her father's world was violent in its own way.

Ashraf sat back and the tautness in her chest eased. When he'd leaned in, capturing her with his intense regard as much as his touch, she had felt ridiculously overwhelmed.

'Qadri was a relic of the past. A criminal who, because his powerbase was in a remote province, was allowed to remain untouched for too long.' Ashraf's mouth thinned. 'My father, the previous Sheikh, had no appetite for tackling intractable problems like ousting a vicious bandit who preyed on his own people. It was too far away from the capital and too hard when there were other, easier initiatives that would win him praise.'

So Ashraf and his father hadn't seen eye to eye? It was there in his voice and the slight upward tilt of his chin. Tori could relate to that.

'So you sent in your soldiers to kill Qadri?' That would explain his violent retaliation.

Ashraf's mouth curled in a small smile. 'Is that how things are done in Australia? In Za'daq the Sheikh upholds the law, rather than breaks it.'

He was laughing at her naivety, making a point about Za'daq being a country as enlightened as hers.

'But, given your experience, it's not surprising you thought otherwise. And it's true that centuries ago the Sheikh would have ridden in with his warriors and slaughtered such a man.'

'So what *did* you do?'

'Deprived him of his powerbase. Introduced schemes to bring the province out of the Dark Ages with adequate power, water and food. Began establishing schools and employment opportunities.' He shook his head. 'I'd only been Sheikh for half a year when we met, and the initiatives were in their infancy, but still they'd had a powerful effect. So had enforcing the law. I had police stationed locally to arrest Qadri's stand-over men when they tried to intimidate people. Qadri realised that soon the people wouldn't see him as the power in the region. They'd have choices and laws they could rely on.'

'So he had you kidnapped?'

'Unfortunately I made it easy, riding with only Basim and a guide into a deserted location to view a new project. The guide was in Qadri's pay.' Another twist of the lips. 'Clearly the security assessment was flawed, but no doubt some would say I was reckless.'

Tori frowned. That didn't gel with the man she knew. He was strong and astute, a strategic thinker and formidably determined.

And he was here for his son.

The reminder was a crackle of frost along her stiff spine.

'You can be assured that Za'daq is now safe to visit. As safe as your country.'

Was that code? His way of telling her that Oliver would be okay in his father's homeland? *Did* he mean to take Oliver from her?

Firming her lips, Tori beat down rising panic. She was jumping to conclusions. No one was going to take her son. There were laws about that. Hadn't Ashraf just taken time to prove he valued the law?

She wondered what the law in Za'daq said about custody of a child. Especially a male child. Was Oliver the Sheikh's heir?

It was no good. She couldn't sit here, pretending this was some polite catch-up with an old acquaintance. The rising burble of her emotions was too unsettling.

'Excuse me.' Tori shot to her feet and paced shakily to the wall of glass. She sensed rather than heard him come up behind her.

'I realise this is overwhelming.'

Tori nodded. She felt as if she'd stepped into a different reality. One where people came back from the dead and where handsome princes mingled with ordinary people.

'Imagine how I felt when I discovered you'd survived. And that you'd had my child.'

Ashraf's voice was low, a caress that tickled her flesh and tightened her nipples. Even after the reality of childbirth and six months of single motherhood, there was something seductively intimate about the way he spoke about her having his baby.

In the window she saw his reflection over her shoulder. His face was sombre, and it struck her for the first time that she wasn't the only one dealing with shock.

She turned to him. 'So where does that leave us?'

He didn't hesitate. 'I want to see Oliver. As soon as possible.'

Naturally. She looked at her watch. It was getting late. 'There's a report I have to complete today. It should only take me another hour.'

Ashraf considered her assessingly. Was he insulted because she didn't instantly jump to do his bidding? Did royal sheikhs ever have to wait for anything?

But he merely nodded. 'An hour, then.'

Two hours later Ashraf paced the sitting room of Tori's small villa, battling impatience and what felt remarkably like nerves.

After sleeping on their way home from the crèche Oliver, his son, had begun to fidget as soon as they'd entered. Ashraf had been torn between the need to reach for the child and wariness because he knew nothing about babies. Except that they were tiny, fragile and totally foreign to his world.

Oliver—the more he used the name, the more he'd get used to it—made him feel too big and clumsy to be trusted with a fragile new life.

Yet none of that had prevented the immediate visceral connection he'd felt. He'd seen a tiny fist wave, caught the gleam of bright dark eyes, and felt emotion pound through his diaphragm strong as a knockout punch.

His son. His flesh and blood.

He'd missed seeing Tori grow big with his baby. He'd missed six months of his child's life. Precious months he could never get back. He had so much to catch up on. So much to learn and experience. And to give. Ashraf would ensure Oliver had the things he'd never had. Paternal love. Tenderness. Trust. Encouragement.

Ashraf would be involved in his son's life. In a positive way.

For a fleeting few seconds it hit him how much his own father had missed by distancing himself from his younger son. By choosing hate and distrust.

But he'd had Ashraf's other brother, Karim. Not that the old man had loved Karim either. Ashraf doubted their father had been capable of love. But he'd taken an interest, encouraged Karim and crowed over his elder son's successes.

A high-pitched grizzle cut into Ashraf's thoughts like an alarm signal resonating through his body. Was something wrong with Oliver?

Fifteen minutes ago Tori had led the way to a small white and yellow room with a cot, a rocking chair and a low bookcase littered with toy animals and little books made of boards. A mat on the floor looked like a farm, with more friendly-faced animals.

Ashraf had never felt so out of place. Especially when Tori had lifted their son high and he'd seen how tiny the mite was without his covering blanket. She'd cast a harried glance at him over her shoulder and suggested he make himself comfortable in the other room while she changed Oliver.

Reluctantly Ashraf had complied. He was curious about the boy but he knew he'd have to give Tori space. He'd thrown a live grenade into her world with his appearance today. He guessed she'd battled traumatic memories since the moment she saw him.

Ashraf frowned. Was it too much to expect her to be pleased to see him? He was used to delighted women… eager women.

For his part, he'd seen her and instantly been swamped

with the need for more. The attraction between them might have started as the product of mortal danger, but it was there still, stronger by the moment.

Then he recalled her breathless reaction when he'd held her hand, the tell-tale tremble and the flutter of long lashes over soft blue eyes. She might not have wanted to feel it but she'd been attracted.

He glanced at his watch. How long did it take to change a nappy? They had things to discuss. He wanted to know his son. He'd allowed her time, even permitted her to stay at work and finish off the project she was so worried about. As if he, Ashraf al Rashid, was of negligible importance.

Ashraf strode down the corridor, knocked once and stepped into the nursery.

Wide eyes brilliant as starlight met his. Then he took in the rest of the scene. Tori in the rocking chair, the baby in her arms. His throat thickened. Her blouse was undone, hanging wide open on one side. A tiny dark head nuzzled at her bare breast.

Ashraf's gaze focused on the voluptuous curve of that breast, on his son's tiny starfish hand patting Tori's alabaster flesh, and heat drenched him from head to toe. The heat of arousal, fierce and primal. A surge of lust erupting with dizzying intensity.

Breastfeeding wasn't something he'd ever thought about. If he had it wouldn't have been in terms of eroticism. Yet, watching the woman he'd made pregnant feed his son, Ashraf had never felt such hungry possessiveness.

'We won't be long.' Tori's voice was husky as she twitched her blouse across to cover herself.

Ashraf nodded.

'He's almost finished.' She looked down, her gaze softening instantaneously on her baby.

Ashraf realised that for all the experience he'd gained in the royal court, in the rigours of army life and in the deliberate hedonism of his globetrotting playboy years, he'd never come across anything as real and fundamental as this.

His son.

His woman.

There wasn't even astonishment. Just calm acceptance. Ashraf hadn't got as far as considering a future wife. He'd been too busy cementing his role in a country that had never expected or wanted the younger, scandalous royal son to inherit.

Besides, this wasn't a matter of logic, but instinct.

He smiled as a glow of satisfaction spread out from his belly.

Tentatively Tori smiled back.

Ashraf felt that smile in places he couldn't even name. He'd never seen her smile before—not properly. He wanted to see her grin, he realised. Hear her laugh. Watch her as their bodies joined and she lost herself to ecstasy. In broad daylight. Not in the murky darkness of a desperate hovel that smelled of terror and pain.

'Ashraf...?' She frowned.

Was she picking up on the anger that simmered in his blood at the memory of what she'd suffered? Or was she frowning from embarrassment at him seeing her feed their child?

He smoothed his expression and leaned against the doorjamb, shoving his hands into his trouser pockets. Tori needed to get used to him being around.

'It's okay. There's no rush. Let him feed.'

Whether it was coincidence, or the sound of his voice, Oliver chose that moment to stop feeding. Ashraf saw a glazed pink nipple before Tori quickly drew her blouse further across. A tiny head turned, dark eyes meeting his.

Ashraf crossed the room in a couple of strides. Oliver tracked the movement. Was that usual for a six-month-old? Or was his son inordinately clever? It was nonsense to think he sensed the link between them. Of course it was.

'Would you like to hold him?' Tori's voice was different, as if she couldn't catch her breath.

'Show me how.'

She demonstrated, supporting the baby and then lifting Oliver up to her shoulder, gently rubbing his back. 'When he's hungry sometimes he gulps down air as well as milk. This helps.'

'I didn't think you'd be breastfeeding when you're working.'

Not that he knew a thing about it. Just that he'd been rooted to the spot by the sight of Tori nursing his child.

'I express milk for him to drink when I'm at work.'

Her cheeks grew pink and Ash stifled the urge to ask exactly what that meant. Time enough later.

'Here.'

She lifted Oliver towards him and suddenly, looking down at the tiny form, Ashraf wasn't so sure about holding him.

Tori read Ashraf's uncertainty and bit back a smile. It was the first time she'd seen him anything but confident. Even facing execution he'd been resolute. And there'd been no mistaking his eagerness when he'd seen Oliver.

That had simultaneously reassured and worried her. She had yet to discover what he intended to do about their son.

Now she read consternation in his bold features as well as…hunger? Her amusement died. Why should their son be any less of a wonder to Ashraf than he was to her? Gently she placed the baby in his arms, holding on longer than necessary while he grew familiar with Oliver's weight.

'Gah,' Oliver said, looking up into the dark, serious face above him. 'Gah-gah.'

'Hello to you too, Oliver Ashal.'

Ashraf's voice held a rough gravelly note that made her insides flutter. When he switched to husky Arabic Tori sank back in the rocker, spellbound by both the lilting sound and the sight of the two males staring into each other's faces.

Ashraf stood stiffly, as if wary of dropping his burden. But gradually he shifted Oliver into a more comfortable hold and Tori's chest squeezed at the contrast between the powerful man and the tiny child. The sight of them tugged at some primitive maternal instinct.

But there was more. Something to do with her feelings for Ashraf. Something that had been there from the start and which, remarkably, was growing stronger.

Tori looked away and focused on doing up her bra and shirt. There was a lot to discuss. Ashraf's appearance from the dead changed so much.

She glanced towards him, her busy hands stilling. Ashraf had Oliver tucked close, as if he'd held him since the day he was born, and the smile he gave his son made Tori's heart wobble. It was radiant.

It made her voice what she'd avoided till now. 'What do you want, Ashraf?'

'Want?'

'From me—us?'

'To be a father to my son.'

'It will take some planning since we live in Australia.' Caution told her not to push this now. But she was on tenterhooks. She needed to know his expectations.

Dark eyes meshed with hers. 'But you don't need to. You could live in Za'daq. Marry me and give our son the life he deserves.'

CHAPTER FIVE

ASHRAF LAY ON his back, staring through the gloom at the bedroom ceiling, and berated himself for his impatience. Being Sheikh often meant holding his tongue and waiting for the right moment to act, persuading people to accept his plans rather than forcing them to follow. Especially since in Za'daq his reputation as both a profligate playboy and his father's all but ignored son meant he battled prejudice and mistrust.

He was used to that. Was used to exerting patience as well as an iron will that stopped his father's old cronies from undermining him too blatantly.

But when Tori had asked what he wanted he hadn't been his usual composed self. He'd been holding his child in his arms for the first time, had felt the uprush of an emotion that nothing had prepared him for. In that moment he'd wanted never to let Oliver go. To ensure his life was better than Ashraf's had been.

Plus there'd been the sight of Tori in her plain white blouse, the buttons done up askew in her haste, tendrils of moonlight-pale hair drifting loose to frame her beguiling face. His heart had whacked his ribs in a rhythm of need, want and determination.

He'd realised his error in the split second it had

taken her expression to close at the idea of marriage and Za'daq.

Now, here he lay, sleepless, seeking the winning argument to overcome her doubts and persuade her to accept what he offered. What was clearly best for their son.

Tori's refusal was a salutary lesson against complacency. He was accustomed to eager women, not women regarding him with suspicion. She probably thought marriage to a sheikh meant she'd be walled up in an old-fashioned harem.

His mouth rucked up at one side. The idea had some appeal. Tori available at his beck and call, reclining with an inviting smile on silk sheets… Heat threaded through his veins and gathered in his groin.

He shifted restlessly. Right now he could be lying in a king-sized bed in the exclusive suite that took up the top floor of Perth's most prestigious hotel. Instead he lay on the carpeted floor of Oliver's room.

Ashraf grunted and rolled onto his side. It was his fault for not treading carefully. For spooking Tori with his abrupt announcement. They'd discussed the matter through the dinner he'd had delivered to her home, and afterwards. But despite her attempt to appear calm he'd read her tension, and the fear he'd done his best to diffuse.

Finally, seeing tiredness in her slumping shoulders, he'd insisted she sleep. But he hadn't been able to leave for his luxury accommodation. It was too soon. He'd just found Oliver, and Tori, and something inside had screeched a protest at the idea of leaving them.

So he'd suggested sleeping on the sofa and Tori had eventually agreed, perhaps because she'd realised she hadn't a hope of shifting him. Apparently Oliver was teething—something Ashraf hadn't even known was a thing—and Tori had admitted broken sleep was taking its toll.

Another reason for him to remain. Tori's refusal to accept the logic of his plan was a nuisance, but seeing her exhausted had made him protective.

As soon as she'd checked on Oliver and gone to her own room Ashraf had taken the bedding she'd put on the too-short sofa and spread it on the floor beside the cot. He'd slept in worse places on army manoeuvres. Besides, this might remind him to think before he spoke.

A cry sounded from the cot and Ashraf shot to his feet. Flicking on the lamp, he peered down to find Oliver's face screwed up and turning red.

Ashraf slipped his hand beneath his squirming son and lifted him to his chest. The baby felt almost familiar this time, his nestling warmth both comforting and a reminder of how scarily fragile he was.

Ashraf inhaled the smell of talc and baby that in a few short hours had become so satisfying. He stilled his thoughts, focusing on the moment. On the wonder of his child, flesh of his flesh. The promise of a fulfilling long life ahead. A life Ashraf was determined to share.

A couple of hours earlier he'd persuaded Oliver back to sleep with gentle words, rocking and a pain-relieving gel rubbed onto his gums. This time he suspected Oliver wouldn't be so easily settled.

Ashraf paced the room, gentling the fractious baby, murmuring soothing words in his own tongue. He wanted to win Tori a little more sleep. The sight of the smudges of tiredness beneath her eyes had made him feel wrong-footed, steaming in and demanding she upend her life to move to Za'daq.

Except that Tori marrying him, creating a family for Oliver and allowing their child to grow up in the country he'd one day rule, was the most important thing. Ashraf's experience as an unwanted child, ostracised by his own father, made him determined to ensure Oliver *belonged*. That he was accepted and given every opportunity to shine.

He'd do whatever it took to persuade Tori, for Oliver's sake.

Tori opened the door and felt her jaw drop. She'd been barely thinking as she'd pushed back the covers and climbed out of bed, blearily acting on instinct when she'd heard Oliver cry. Now she was fully awake, and staring.

Ash...Ashraf...filled the room, tall, athletically built and almost naked. His wide shoulders and bare back gleamed, a symphony of muscle overlaid with burnished satin skin. Tori's throat closed as her gaze tracked his spine, moved down long, powerful legs, then up to navy underwear that clung to rounded buttocks. Near his feet lay the pillow and bedding she'd put on the sofa.

He'd slept on Oliver's floor.

The idea stunned her as much as the sight of Ashraf, overwhelmingly virile and masculine, in her private space.

Then there was the way he rocked from side to side, cradling Oliver against his shoulder. Ashraf's voice was a soft, deep hum as he sang a lullaby in a language she didn't understand. It didn't seem to be working on Oliver, who still fretted. But it worked on her. Tori swayed and reached for the doorjamb to prop herself up, her insides turning to mush at the combination of supercharged sexy male and breath-stealing tenderness.

For a dangerous moment she let herself imagine what it would be like if they were a real family—not as Ashraf suggested, for convenience, but because they loved—

No. She wasn't going there. She'd got this far as a single mother and knew she could manage it. Dreams were all well and good but she couldn't confuse them with reality.

'I think you'd better give him to me.'

Ashraf swung round and Tori was hit by another pulse of—okay, she'd admit it—arousal. He was a truly magnificent man, and the sight of her little son secure against that broad bare chest sent emotion curvetting through her.

Tori blamed overactive hormones. And weariness. But then she read Ashraf's expression and thoughts of herself faded. In those strong features and glittering eyes was a reflection of her own feelings when she surveyed Oliver. Wonder, love and protectiveness.

Ashraf might be new to fatherhood, but that didn't mean his feelings for Oliver were less real. Or that he had a smaller claim to parenthood.

The knowledge rushed at her like a biting wind, piercing the mental armour with which she'd shielded her fears. She'd told herself Oliver was *hers*. That because she barely knew Ashraf, that he came from a faraway place and a time in her life best forgotten, his claim on the baby was less.

How untrue that was. This man, who ruled a country and probably slept in a gilded bed with silk sheets, surrounded by every luxury, had bunked down on the hard floor beside his son. That hadn't been done to make a point.

'Tori! Are you okay?' Ashraf stepped close in a couple of long strides, one warm hand closing around her elbow. 'You look unsteady on your feet.'

She shook her head, pushing her hair back from her face, and stood straighter. 'I'm all right.' As all right as she could be when her life had suffered a sudden seismic shift.

As if from a huge distance she saw her plans for a new life in Perth fracture. Whatever the future held, it wasn't going to be as straightforward as she'd expected.

Ashraf led her to the rocking chair, his hold supportive and expression serious. When Tori experienced another jolt of awareness she felt like a fraud. Then, when he leaned close to pass Oliver over, the warm, evocative scent of spiced cinnamon and male flesh surrounded her. Her nipples tingled, and it wasn't just reaction to Oliver's hungry cry. It was connected to the pulsing throb low in her body.

She shivered and tightened her hold on her baby.

'You're cold?'

The words trawled over her bare arms like a velvet ribbon.

No, she was burning up.

How could she react so viscerally to a man she barely knew? She wasn't by nature promiscuous. Yet with Ashraf...

She'd told herself that what had happened that night in Za'daq had happened because they'd been in mortal danger. That they'd been driven by a primal impulse to procreate and ensure the survival of another generation. What excuse did she have now?

It was as if she was wired to respond instantly and catastrophically to Ashraf.

'No, not cold. Just tired.'

'I'll get you a hot drink. You need to replace fluids.'

Then, before she could stop him, he strode out of the room.

Ashraf spent as long as he could in the kitchen. Anything to stay away from Tori and regroup.

She'd stood in the doorway, looking dazed and delicate, and he'd been torn between concern and fascination at how the hall light behind her outlined her tantalising shape through her nightdress. Pouting breasts, narrow waist, long, slender legs and gently rounded hips.

He'd wanted to grab her hard against him. Need had clawed, urgent and unstoppable.

Her hair was a messy halo, her cheeks flushed. Her lemon-yellow nightgown had a row of buttons down the front, presumably to make breastfeeding easier. Only a couple of those prim buttons had been fastened, allowing him tantalising glimpses of pearly skin.

Memories of losing himself in Tori's sweet body bombarded him, of her soft cries of encouragement and the incredible bliss of a coupling that had far transcended the brutal reality of that foul kidnappers' hut.

He frowned and moved to the kettle, filling it with water. His years of scandalous indulgence might have been designed to infuriate his father, but they hadn't been a complete sham—even if his sexual exploits *had* been exaggerated. He was used to sophisticated women well versed in seductive wiles. He was used to silk, satin and lace, or complete nudity. Not dainty cotton with embroidered flowers. Not nursing mothers.

Ashraf shook his head and straightened. Nothing about this trip was going to plan. But he was adaptable. He had no intention of leaving without his son. Or Tori.

Tori had finished feeding Oliver but Ashraf still hadn't returned. Had he thought better of spending the night there? The possibility made her feel curiously bereft. But sneaking off without declaring his intentions wasn't Ashraf's style.

'Shall we swap?'

At the sound of his low voice she swung round, hugging Oliver close.

Far from planning to leave, Ashraf hadn't even bothered to dress. Tori's skin tingled with a blush as she fought to stop her gaze going lower than the mug he held.

She'd never been particularly bashful, and until today rarely blushed. Maybe that was due to her father's demands that she accompany him to public events from an early age. Or because female geologists were still outnumbered by men. As a result she'd learned to hide anything that might be viewed as feminine weakness.

Ashraf put the steaming mug down on a chest of drawers and reached for Oliver.

'He's almost asleep.' Tori hugged him closer, as if the baby could protect her from unwanted feelings.

'Good. I'll hold him for a little, then put him down while you have your drink.'

Remembering the look on Ashraf's face as he'd watched Oliver, how could she resist? Tori passed the baby to him, supremely conscious of her nakedness under her nightie and Ashraf's bare arms brushing hers.

Not that Ashraf noticed. His attention was all on Oliver as he paced to the window, stroking the baby's head with one big hand. Something dipped hard in Tori's chest and she turned away, picking up the mug and taking a sip as she sat down.

'This is good!'

'No need to sound surprised. Even kings can boil water.'

She liked the teasing lilt in his voice too much.

'I expected tea.'

Dark eyebrows lifted as he caught her eye then turned away, rocking Oliver. 'I didn't know how you took it, and I didn't want to interrupt, so I made my own favourite.'

'Lemon, honey and…' she paused, taking another sip '…fresh ginger?' So simple yet so delicious.

He nodded, but kept his gaze on their son.

Tori drew a shaky breath and confronted the reality she'd fought from the moment Ashraf had told her his intentions.

'I've been thinking.'

'Yes?'

His head lifted, gleaming eyes pinioning her. It didn't matter that Ashraf was more than half naked and holding a sleeping baby. He looked as powerful as any sovereign in full royal regalia.

Anxiety feathered her spine but she kept her gaze on his, refusing to be intimidated.

'I can't marry you.' She watched the corners of his mouth fold in, as if he was holding back an objection. 'But I understand your desire, your *right* to be involved in Oliver's life.' Her heart pattered faster as she made herself continue. 'I'm still not sure about him being a prince, though. Surely when you eventually marry your legitimate children will inherit?'

'I told you I can legitimise Oliver. I intend to. And I have no intention of taking any other wife.'

Heat flashed through her like a channel of lava, incinerating more of her defences. It shouldn't make a difference, but when Ashraf spoke like that part of her enjoyed it—though it was ludicrous to believe he cared about her as anything other than Oliver's mother.

Of course he'd marry. Some glamorous princess who'd charm his people and give him a bevy of children.

Something sharp lodged in Tori's ribs and she had to breathe slowly to ease the spike of discomfort.

'I'm not entirely convinced becoming Crown Prince of Za'daq is what I want for him.'

Ashraf's brow corrugated and his mouth tightened. Tori wondered what he wasn't saying. That it wasn't up to her to decide such things?

'Because you believe my country is unsafe? That's understandable, given your abduction, but believe me, that's not the case now.'

'That's part of it, but not all.'

How did she even begin to express her horror at the idea of her precious boy being thrust into such a public role with no choice? She'd spent her childhood and teenage years as a handy asset in her father's politicking. She'd hated it—especially as she'd got old enough to understand his cynical use of a good photo opportunity and his focus on self-aggrandisement rather than public service.

'I want Oliver to have the opportunity to be a child

just like any other.' Not shunted around to smile for the press when the polls looked bad or family values were a hot issue for voters.

'Oliver will have that. You have my word.'

'You've said he's destined to become Sheikh. What if he doesn't want to be?'

The idea of her little baby inheriting seemed impossible. Ashraf was so vital and strong. Tori's insides squeezed at the idea of him dying. But he'd come close just last year.

'That's what you're worried about?' He shook his head and the lamplight caught indigo shadows in his inky hair. 'Most women would be thrilled at the idea of their child inheriting riches and power.'

'Most women don't have a politician for a father. Power shouldn't be an end in itself.' She paused, weighing her words. 'It can have a negative effect on a person and on those around them.'

Her father would say he did what he did for the public good. Tori knew he was driven instead by the need for acclaim and power. He was self-serving, and as a father...

'You're right. Power is an obligation.' Ashraf studied her intently as if fascinated by a new insight.

Tori wished she had more than her nightie and a hot drink to shield her from that penetrating gaze.

Conditioned by a lifetime's training, she found it hard to admit aloud her negative feelings about her father and his profession. But this was about Oliver. Nothing, not even the ingrained habit of old loyalty, took precedence.

'Yet you want to tie our child to that before he's even old enough to understand!' She wanted to grab the now sleeping baby and tuck him close. Her fingers clamped hard around the warm mug.

Ashraf's features tightened, the proud lines of nose and forehead growing more defined. 'I will give Oliver the opportunity to inherit what is his right as my son. To lead the people of Za'daq is an honour as well as a responsibility. I won't deprive him of his birthright.'

For a long, pulsing moment Ashraf's eyes bored into hers and she felt her breath clog in her lungs. He was formidable. Daunting. Yet still she felt the fizz of attraction like effervescence in her blood.

Biased by seeing her father and his cronies at close quarters, Tori had told herself she disliked powerful men. But strength was intrinsic to Ashraf and still she was drawn, fascinated, even as her saner self warned her to keep her distance.

'There's always a choice, Tori. No one will force Oliver if he truly doesn't want to become Sheikh. My brother, Karim, was heir to the throne. Yet when my father died Karim declined his inheritance. I was proclaimed Sheikh instead.'

Tori wanted to ask *why* Karim had chosen not to inherit. What he was doing now. Had Ashraf wanted the throne? But the stern set of his mouth warned against questions.

'Surely it's not too much to give our son the opportunity to learn the ways of his forebears? To have access to both cultures—Za'daqi and Australian.'

'I agree.'

'You do?' The fierce glitter in his eyes softened.

'I told you I'd been thinking.'

She swallowed, her stomach churning at what she'd

decided. But she had to follow through. It would be cowardly and selfish not to.

'I have serious doubts about the Sheikh thing…' Ashraf's eyebrows rose, yet he didn't interrupt. 'But I'm willing to accept your suggestion. *Not* to marry,' she hurried to clarify, 'but to take Oliver to Za'daq for a visit.'

She read no change in Ashraf's features. No smile, no lessening in the intensity of that stare. But the next breath he drew was so deep it lifted that mighty chest like a cresting ocean wave.

'Thank you, Tori.' He stepped close, one arm effortlessly holding Oliver, the other reaching for her.

She stumbled to her feet, feeling at a disadvantage in the low rocking chair.

Ashraf took her hand, and the hard, enveloping warmth reminded her of the physical differences between them. Differences that, to her dismay, made her body hum and soften.

Instead of shaking her hand, he lifted it. 'You are generous as well as wise and beautiful.'

Tori blinked, and would have tugged free of his grasp except, still holding her gaze, he pressed his lips to the back of her hand. Instantly energy arced from the spot, shooting to her breasts, her pelvis, right down to her toes.

'There's no need to soft-soap me.'

'Soft-soap?'

For the first time Ashraf looked out of his depth. Tori enjoyed that puzzled expression. It was rather endearing. For once she didn't feel as if she were the one playing catch up.

'Flatter me,' she explained.

'I never flatter. I simply speak the truth.'

Which trashed her fleeting sense of superiority.

She stood, her hand in his, staring up into liquid dark eyes and wishing—

What? Wishing that they'd met under different circumstances? Ashraf would still be a king and therefore not the man for her. Wishing that he was someone altogether different? Some guy she'd met at a weekend barbecue? But she couldn't imagine that. Ashraf's identity was part of what made him intriguing.

But it wasn't the forceful, charismatic side of his personality that had made her change her mind. It was his genuine interest in Oliver. His determination to be a meaningful part of his son's life even if that meant waking in the night and walking the floor with a teething baby. One thing she was sure of: Ashraf wouldn't be a father who only showed up for the fun stuff. He'd be there through thick and thin.

Oliver deserved no less. Therefore Ashraf deserved more.

Belatedly she realised he still held her hand. She slipped it free. 'Don't get too excited. It will take me a while to organise. I've only recently begun this job and—'

'Getting leave from your work will be no problem.'

Tori's hackles rose. 'You haven't already asked without consulting me, have you?'

She saw him register her rising indignation. *Good.* She had no intention of being railroaded.

Ashraf shook his head. 'I know the CEO of your company. He's interested in exploring for diamonds in Za'daq.'

Tori wasn't surprised. The possibility of finding diamonds and other gems in the region was what had taken her to the survey team in neighbouring Assara. That experience was part of the reason she'd won her current position.

'He knows it was you I came to meet. I'm sure, if I indicate that his company can bid for the upcoming exploration contract, he'd believe it worthwhile to give you leave of absence.'

Tori opened her mouth, then shut it again. Of course he would. The company would probably pay her airfare and keep her on full pay indefinitely!

She felt cornered. She'd counted on having more time before taking Oliver to Za'daq. A year, perhaps.

'I need to sort out a passport for Oliver.'

'No problem. I can expedite that.'

Tori stared up at the big man holding their son and unease slipped down her spine. She reached out and took Oliver, hugging him close before putting him in his cot. The comfort of his tiny body against hers eased her nerves. No one would steal her son. Yet she took her time, trailing her knuckle over his satiny cheek, feeling her heart lurch as he turned towards her touch.

Breathing deep, she straightened. 'You've already made enquiries, haven't you?'

Ashraf's expression confirmed it.

'You haven't got him a passport already?'

'I cannot without your consent. But my staff have checked with the Australian authorities and there's no problem.' He paused. 'I cancelled my schedule to come here but I need to return soon. We can leave tomorrow.'

'Tomorrow!' Tori crossed her arms over her body, holding in rising panic. 'That's impossible.'

He spread his hands in a gesture that might have

seemed apologetic if not for the look of satisfaction on his face. 'One of the perks of being a visiting head of state…' His expression grew sombre. 'You don't appear happy to have these impediments removed. Didn't you mean it about bringing Oliver to Za'daq?'

'Of course I did.' She rubbed her hands up her arms. 'I just didn't expect things to move so fast. And…' She chewed her lip.

'And…? Something's bothering you? What is it?' His gaze probed. 'Tell me, Tori. I can't deal with the problem if I don't know what it is.'

She hitched a breath. 'I feel you're taking control. As if I have no say. That makes me wonder how much power I'll have in Za'daq.' She angled her chin. 'Whether you'll have the power to take Oliver from me there.'

Ashraf read Tori's fear and guilt scrolled like an unwinding roll of calligraphy through his belly.

Of course she was concerned. She'd be crazy not to worry. It was true. In Za'daq, once he'd claimed Oliver as his heir, Ashraf would have the authority to keep his son permanently. Just as he'd have the ability to keep Tori within his borders or, alternatively, have her deported.

Ashraf refused to countenance Oliver living half a world away. He'd do whatever it took to have his son with him, where he belonged. Marrying Tori would ensure that. But their future together would be most successful if Tori *chose* to marry. If she *wanted* it.

Oh, she wanted him. He'd read her physical response. But persuading a woman like Tori into marriage would take patience and finesse.

Or an all-out assault on her senses.

Ashraf considered seducing her here and now. Till he remembered her concern to do the right thing by him and Oliver. He owed her more than that. Even though he was impatient for their physical union.

She spoke of a visit to his country, whereas he intended to keep Tori and Oliver with him in Za'daq. Permanently. That would require a concerted attack on Tori's doubts and defences. Showing her how much his homeland had to offer, how much *he* could offer.

'You have my word. On my family name and my country's honour I won't keep you or Oliver in Za'daq if you wish to leave.'

Ashraf's mouth curved. He looked forward to convincing her to stay.

CHAPTER SIX

Two DAYS LATER Tori peered through the window of Ashraf's private jet, taking in tawny desert plains far below and misty blue-smudged mountains in the distance.

If it wasn't for the high ridge of mountains this might be central Australia's vast arid zone. But the tension prickling her skin belied the comparison.

This was where she'd been kidnapped.

Where those men—

Ashraf's hand covered hers where it gripped the armrest. His touch quelled the shudder ripping through her.

'Okay, Tori?'

She wasn't. She'd told herself she could do this, that it was right to do this. But at the sight of the desert she felt terrifying memories stir. Distress prickled the back of her eyes and she feared she'd lose the exquisitely prepared meal she'd just eaten.

'Of course.' She blinked, keeping her focus on the view as the shudder reduced to a rippling undercurrent of unease. 'It can't be long till we land.'

Ashraf said nothing. He must have registered her anxiety, yet instead of pulling back and following her lead in the change of subject he leaned closer, his warmth penetrating through her jacket and shirt.

Tori caught her bottom lip, stunned at how needy she felt for more. Even now, when fraught memories threatened her fragile composure.

Ashraf's breath caressed her cheek as he pointed to the mountains in the distance. 'Those foothills mark the border territory between Za'daq and Assara. You were abducted there, then brought to the encampment on this side of the border.'

Tori didn't want to think about it. Yet she craned towards the window.

'Then you crossed back into Assara. No wonder we couldn't find a trace of you. If you'd worked in Za'daq we'd at least have been able to identify you through your work visa.'

Tori wasn't interested in unmarked borders or the state of record-keeping in the neighbouring country of Assara. She stared at the sharply folded hills and her stomach swooped.

'The people there are very poor,' he went on. 'That's one of the reasons I'm considering allowing mineral exploration in the region.'

'Mining doesn't necessarily lead to money for the locals. Some are employed for minimum wages but most companies bring in their own expertise.'

She worked in the industry but that didn't mean she was blind to its flaws.

'It depends on the terms negotiated,' Ashraf responded. 'Nothing will be endorsed unless it provides decent local employment and infrastructure. Profits will be channelled into regional initiatives.'

Tori blinked. In her experience profits went to wealthy investors, making them wealthier.

'That's very admirable.'

His fingers tightened, reminding her that he still held her hand. Then he withdrew, leaving her feeling ridiculously bereft.

'You thought my interest was for personal gain?' Ashraf's lovely deep voice sounded different. Distant. Or perhaps affronted.

'No.' She swung round to meet his stare. 'I—'

'It's fine, Tori.'

Though when he said her name it wasn't with the warmth she'd become accustomed to.

'It's what many will think—that I'm looking for riches to spend on myself rather than the public good.'

No mistaking his bitterness.

'But contrary to popular opinion my focus is my people, not myself.'

She was intrigued—not only by his words but also by the hint of vulnerability she'd sensed at his withdrawal. It belied the haughty cast of his expression.

'Your people believe you're not interested in them?'

He shrugged, those wide shoulders spreading. 'Many do. Or at least…' He paused, as if choosing his words. 'I spent several years scandalising polite society with my "reckless, self-absorbed, self-indulgent lifestyle". Some find it hard to believe that's over.'

Anxiety forgotten, Tori twisted towards him. 'That sounds like a quote.'

'Sorry?' His eyebrows crinkled in confusion.

'The bit about being reckless and self-indulgent. It sounded like someone else's words.'

Ashraf's eyes widened and she read his surprise.

Then his gaze became shuttered. Clearly this wasn't something he'd allow her to pursue. But whose words had made such an impression?

'You're not reckless and self-indulgent now.'

It wasn't a question. How could it be when Tori had first-hand experience of Ashraf's character? He'd tried to protect her in the desert. He'd searched for her for over a year, never giving up. He'd accepted his role as Oliver's father without question, without even hinting about the need for a paternity test. No avoidance or denial, just unflinching acceptance of the circumstances and a determination to do the best he could.

One black eyebrow rose as if he doubted her assessment.

'Well, you're not.'

It was true that he'd been notorious—as Tori had discovered when she trawled the Internet. But for the last two years he'd barely been out of Za'daq. Every photo showed a serious, almost grim man, usually surrounded by a flock of courtiers or regional leaders. News reports about him focused on social and political issues, regional trade discussions, health improvements and so on.

However, older reports revealed that the younger Ashraf had lived a lifestyle that kept the paparazzi on its toes.

Skiing at the trendiest resorts, escaping to fabled islands in the Pacific and the Caribbean, frequenting exclusive clubs, casinos and the sort of parties that fuelled the media's insatiable appetite for gossip.

She'd found photos that had made her stare. Prince Ashraf stumbling out of a casino in the early hours, accompanied by not one glamorous model but three, all looking as if they'd like to eat him for breakfast. A long-distance shot of him diving, naked, off a billion-aire's yacht after a week-long party. Even the grainy quality of the shot hadn't disguised his taut, powerful frame, and Tori's pulse had tripped to a rackety beat.

'You sound very sure of my character,' he murmured, and she couldn't work out if he was annoyed, intrigued or merely making an observation.

Tori shrugged, turning to the view. This time those rugged hills didn't fill her with quite the same dread, though she still found herself clasping her hands tight.

'There's a lot I don't know about you, Ashraf, but we've shared some intense experiences. Self-absorbed isn't how I'd describe you.'

'How *would* you describe me?' he asked after a heartbeat's silence.

Tori sucked in a breath.

Magnetic. Sexy. Disturbing.

And one step ahead of her since the moment he'd confronted her in Perth. Tori felt she was playing catch-up with someone who knew the rules in a game she had yet to learn. And yet...

'Decisive. Obstinate, but with a well-developed sense of responsibility. Used to getting your own way.'

Tori heard a crack of laughter but refused to look at him. She'd seen him smile, felt the full force of his at-tractiveness, and wasn't ready to face it again. Not when she was so out of her depth.

'If only that were true. Being Sheikh means temper-ing my impatience for change so I can persuade others to see my vision for the future.'

Curious, unable to resist, she finally turned, noting

the tiny lines bracketing his firm mouth. Lines that spoke of weariness and restraint.

'I thought the Sheikh of Za'daq had absolute power? Can't you just make a decree?'

'You've done your homework.'

'A little. I haven't had time to discover much.'

Again Tori experienced that plunging sensation in her stomach. Everything had happened so quickly.

'There's plenty of time to learn all you want to.' He paused, ebony eyes resting on her in a way that made the blood sizzle under her skin. 'And you're right. Technically I have the power to do as I wish. But in practice the Sheikh works with the Royal Council, which is made up of powerful provincial leaders. It would be madness to institute major change without bringing the Council on board.'

His tone was easy but Tori sensed strong emotion ruthlessly repressed. Or perhaps she was making something from nothing. Essentially he was a stranger. Surely it was crazy to believe she could read him.

Tori tugged her gaze back to the view.

'It's true, you know…'

His voice dropped, holding a low, resonant note that ran through her like warm treacle.

'The border province is peaceful now. You have nothing to fear in Za'daq. You and Oliver are safe in my country.'

Safe? Protected from marauding bandits, perhaps. But Tori knew with a shiver of premonition that the most perilous threat came from the man beside her. The man determined to raise Oliver as a Za'daqi prince. The man who'd turned her world on its head and undermined all her certainties.

* * *

She was glad of Ashraf's supporting hand as the plane's door was opened to reveal steps down to the Tarmac. For as they emerged bright sunlight engulfed them, and with it the scent of the desert.

A tremor of panic racked her, making her shake all over, gluing her soles to the top of the steps. Rough fingers seemed to scrabble up her nape then curl around her windpipe, crushing the flow of air.

It should be impossible to smell anything other than aviation fuel and the warm cinnamon notes of Ashraf's skin as he stood close. Yet her nostrils twitched, inhaling the faint scents of dry earth and indefinable spice she associated with the desert.

Instead of hurrying her down the stairs Ashraf stood unmoving, his hand firm at her elbow, giving her time to take it all in. The airport building to one side. Cars at the foot of the steps, where a knot of people waited. Hangars, aircraft. And beyond that, just visible over a collection of modern buildings, arid brown earth.

Tori inhaled sharply, fear stabbing her chest. Her arms tightened around her sleeping son and the pulse of her blood became a panicked flurry in her ears.

Ashraf spoke. She heard the reassuring murmur of his voice, felt his gaze on her face, and finally managed another breath, steadier this time.

Eventually his words began to penetrate. A gentle flow describing the new airport building, finished last year. The recent economic boost as Za'daq had capitalised on its location to become a regional transport hub. The businesses clustered around the airport as a result.

Another listener would have heard a sheikh proud of his country. But Tori, catching his eye as her body finally unfroze, saw concern glimmer in those black eyes. A whump of emotion hit her. Like the invisible force-field of an explosion that would have knocked her off her feet if he hadn't held her.

He knows. He understands.

There was no impatience in those strong features. Just reassurance to counter the chill that defied the blaze of sunlight and turned her bones brittle.

Had he expected her to panic? Tori had been nervous, but nothing had prepared her for the sudden freezing dread.

She took a breath, then another. This time Ashraf's warm scent filled her nostrils, and Oliver's comforting clean baby smell. Tori licked her lips, moistening her mouth. Ashraf followed the movement and heat of another kind flared.

'So much development in such a short space of time,' she murmured, her voice husky. 'It must have taken a lot of work.'

It wasn't an insightful observation but it was the best she could do. Ashraf nodded. He appeared relaxed, yet Tori felt the tension in his tall frame, as if he was ready at any moment to gather up both her and Oliver. His eyes flickered to the baby and Tori read his unspoken question.

But with his help her panic had passed. Her knees had stopped wobbling and her hold on Oliver was firm. She inclined her head and Ashraf turned towards the steps and the group of people watching.

He led the way, taking his time as he spoke about the long-term vision to make Za'daq a centre for communications and information technology.

Neither the aircraft crew nor the people by the limousines would have guessed at Tori's sickening wave of fear. Gratitude filled her for Ashraf's support. Especially when they finally reached the Tarmac and she read the barely veiled disapproval on some of the faces turned her way.

An older man approached and bowed. The bow spoke of deference, but the dismissive glance he cast her and Oliver spoke volumes. It shored up her determination to stand tall.

Ashraf frowned as the man spoke. His voice was no longer mellifluous and reassuring as he asked the man a question, then another, in the same language.

A short time later, after a few brisk words from Ashraf, the entourage retreated to the limousines.

'I'm sorry,' he said, turning to her. 'Something has come up which requires my attention. I won't accompany you to the palace. But you'll be well looked after.' He gestured towards a slight gangly figure in a pale grey robe who, instead of retreating with the others, stepped forward. 'Bram will see you settled.'

This man also bowed to Ashraf, but then turned and bowed to her too. 'Ms Nilsson.'

He straightened and Tori looked into a pair of blue eyes, startling against swarthy skin.

'It's a pleasure to meet you.'

'And you...Bram.' Had she heard that right? She'd thought it an Irish name.

He smiled, his mouth hitching higher at one side because of a long scar cleaving his cheek. 'This way, please.'

Tori peered up at Ashraf. He was her only anchor in this foreign place. She battled the impulse to clutch him. That impulse was far too strong.

Ashraf opened his mouth to speak again but she forestalled him. 'It will be good to get Oliver settled.' Their son was awake now, waving one tiny hand. Soon he'd be demanding a feed.

The predictability of his needs helped ground her. Nothing was more important than Oliver. So, within minutes of arriving in Za'daq, she and her son were on their way to the capital while Ashraf attended to his important business.

Bram, in the front beside the driver, turned with that lopsided smile. 'There's our destination. The royal palace.'

Tori's nerves jangled as she stared. Of *course* a king would live in a palace. She'd had so much on her mind she hadn't considered that.

The palace sprawled magnificently across a hill above the city. Its acres of white stone gleamed in the sun, making it visible well beyond the city fringe.

From a distance its size and pristine colour caught the eye, and then its fairy-tale towers and gilded domes. Eventually, as the limousine climbed a road lined with public parks, Tori felt her breath catch at the palace's sheer beauty. There was carved marble, patterns of lustrous tiles worked in deep blues, greens and golds. Even the intricate ironwork of the tall fence pleased the eye.

Yet Tori's skin turned clammy. *This* was Ashraf's home? The place he wanted her and Oliver to live? This was a palace for a potentate, proclaiming wealth and power. Despite its beauty, it sent a shudder through her.

It didn't matter that they were only visiting, or that he hadn't mentioned marriage again. She suspected Ashraf wasn't a man who'd easily give up when he had his mind fixed on an idea. If they were to agree on some way of sharing Oliver this place would become a significant part of her son's life and therefore hers.

As the daughter of a senior politician she'd attended functions at luxury hotels and private venues, but never anywhere like this.

She looked down at the slate-blue trousers and jacket she'd thought so perfect for travelling and felt completely out of her depth. But how *did* one dress for a palace straight out of a fairy tale?

A bubble of panicked laughter rose as she tried to imagine herself bedecked in glittering gems or ermine or whatever it was that royals wore in places like this.

If Ashraf were here beside her it would be easier.

Even thinking that felt like a betrayal. Tori had always stood up for herself and it was especially important that she do so now. Ashraf and his managing ways had swept her back to a country where she'd never wanted to venture again.

Once more icy fingers played up her spine. Had she made the biggest mistake ever, coming here? She'd agreed to come when she'd been tired and stressed, thrown by seeing Ashraf again when she'd believed him dead.

She'd experienced a destabilising uprush of emotions on seeing him so caring of Oliver, so charismatic that her heart had fluttered in a ridiculous butterfly beat high in her throat. That toned, muscle-packed body, those incredible eyes that seemed to see more of her private self than anyone ever had. Even the thin scar along his ribs that told the story of their near-death experience made her feel close to him. As if they shared something profound.

Tori huffed a silent laugh. They did share something significant. Oliver.

Of course she'd done right in coming here. This was a first step in coming to an agreement about how their son would be raised.

Tori's gaze slewed back to the dazzling white edifice taking up the whole hilltop, her hands clenching. She needed some space after days and nights in Ashraf's company. Yet...*she missed him*.

Tori's eyes widened.

How long since Ashraf had prowled the length of the Perth boardroom and her heart had taken off like a rocket? A mere couple of days since he'd blasted her life to smithereens.

The limousine swung past the palace's monumental main gates and followed a road around the perimeter, eventually pulling in to a more utilitarian entrance.

A uniformed servant opened her door. By the time she'd picked up Oliver and stepped out Bram was urging her inside.

Out of the air-conditioned car, with Oliver warm in her arms, she felt flushed and crumpled. But pride made her stand straight as she was introduced to the palace chamberlain, a tall man in snowy robes.

Gathering her wits, she did what she'd failed to do on meeting Bram, exchanging greetings in Arabic. She knew just enough to understand his wish that she would be comfortable during her stay and to thank him in the same language.

Was that surprise in his eyes? She didn't have time to find out, for Bram was ushering her into a cool, beautifully tiled hall.

'Your apartment is here, at the rear of the palace.'

After turning into another hallway, even more lavishly decorated, and through a courtyard filled with the scent of lilies, he opened a door and invited her to precede him.

Tori stopped dead a few paces in.

'A maid has been assigned to you, and a nanny to help—' Bram's words halted as he saw her face. 'Is the suite not suitable? If not I—'

'It's perfectly suitable, thank you.'

Tori dragged her eyes from the domed ceiling with its mosaic tiles depicting an idyllic garden filled with flowers. The glittering background tiles couldn't be real gold, she told herself. As for the elegant sofas and the beautiful, delicately carved side tables and the pots of colourful orchids… It was impossibly luxurious and gorgeous.

Tori felt simultaneously out of place and desperate to flop down on one of those pale couches and close her eyes.

The sound of water caught her ears and she turned. Tall, arched windows gave on to another courtyard where water sprayed in jets beside a long, inviting pool.

'There's a cot in the second bedroom and a range of baby supplies. If anything is missing you just need to ask the maid or pick up the phone. I can personally—'

Tori roused herself from her daze. 'I'm sure we'll have everything we need. Thank you, Bram. You've been most kind.'

Twenty minutes later she was feeding Oliver, seated in a deeply upholstered chair so comfortable it felt as if her bones melted into it. Her luggage had been unpacked for her. At her side was a frosted glass of juice and an array of mouthwatering pastries brought by a friendly maid.

She was surrounded by luxury, by people eager to please. And yet as she surveyed her sumptuous surroundings Tori wondered if she'd walked into a trap.

A trap devised by a man intent on securing his son at any cost.

CHAPTER SEVEN

'THERE'S ALREADY CONJECTURE about Ms Nilsson.'

'So soon?' Ashraf met Bram's eyes. The rumour mill around the royal court was more efficient than any modern communication software. 'I should have expected it.' Yet he'd convinced himself they had more time.

He rolled his head from side to side, feeling the ache in his neck from too many sleepless hours. They faced a full-blown public scandal when the truth of Tori's and Oliver's identities were known. Yet he had no regrets. How could he have done anything other than bring Oliver and his mother here?

Bram spread his hands. 'Once the Minister for the Interior heard you had a female companion—'

'He manufactured a reason to meet the plane.' The Minister had been a friend of Ashraf's father. He'd absorbed the old Sheikh's disdain for Ashraf and now waited—daily, it seemed—for his new King to take a false step.

Ashraf wasn't naïve. He knew the powerful men who'd formed his father's innermost clique still harboured hopes that something would go wrong. That *he'd* go wrong and then his brother, Karim, would return to take the crown.

That would never happen.

Karim's reason for rejecting the crown was insurmountable. Karim would return to Za'daq one day, but only to visit. He'd made that clear. Only the two brothers knew the real reason for his refusal to become Sheikh, and Ashraf cared for Karim too much ever to betray that secret. Not even to squash the machinations of those trying to destabilise his rule.

He was more than capable of dealing with them. Life had made him more resilient and determined than those waiting for him to fail. As for being underestimated… they'd learn. Ashraf wouldn't countenance failure. He'd never been good enough for his old man but he was determined to be the Sheikh his country needed, no matter what the political establishment thought.

'If it's any consolation,' Bram went on, 'we discovered who leaked the news that you had a travel companion. Someone in the palace administrative team. He's been dismissed.'

Bram paused, frowning, presumably at the knowledge that it was someone in his own unit who'd breached confidentiality.

'But this morning I offered him an alternative job, in the outer provinces, coordinating the infant immunisation campaign. It will give him a chance to put his talent for disseminating information to good use.'

Ashraf felt a smile tug his mouth. 'You think he'll do well there?' The rural location would challenge someone used to city life.

Bram spread his hands. 'I said if he did an outstanding job, meeting all our targets for immunisation over the next three years, I *might* be able to persuade you not to prosecute him for breach of privacy.'

Ashraf's smile became a grin. 'Trust you to turn a problem into an opportunity.'

His old friend was an expert at that—possibly because he'd had so much experience at picking himself up and moving on, no matter what life threw at him.

Bram shrugged. 'He's got talent. It would be a shame to waste it. As for fixing problems—that's what you pay me for.'

'We need to change your job title from Royal Secretary to Chief Troubleshooter!'

Ashraf would have sacked the palace employee and washed his hands of the man. But then, as his father had enjoyed pointing out, Ashraf was his impulsive son.

Over the years he'd changed that, learning in the military to think strategically as well as quickly. But sometimes his desire for swift action led to complications. Like taking a too-quick security assessment at face value, riding into bandit territory and getting kidnapped...

He rubbed a palm around the back of his neck.

'The news is contained for now,' said Bram. 'No one knows the truth about Ms Nilsson or the boy. Just that they're here.'

Ashraf nodded. 'I want it to stay that way as long as possible.' And it wasn't just that he needed time to persuade Tori into marriage. 'We need to suppress the story of how we met. Permanently.'

'Of course. Admitting you were kidnapped within our borders—'

'It's not just that.' Though such news wouldn't do his standing any good. 'She'd be horribly embarrassed if all the world knew just when and where our son was conceived.'

Ashraf's time with Tori had been a pure blessing in the midst of what he'd imagined would be his final painful hours on earth. He didn't want the press or his father's cronies discovering the details and turning them into salacious gossip, so the world could picture Tori giving herself to him in that foul prison filled with the stink of past torture and brutality.

A shiver scudded down his spine and Ashraf's mouth firmed. If nothing else, he'd save her that.

'When the time comes the world can know that we met and I fathered a child. But as for anything else—' He sliced the possibility off with a swift lopping motion.

'You're shielding her?'

'Of course.'

Bram nodded, but Ashraf knew from the speculative gleam in his eyes that he was processing his friend's protectiveness.

'We should be able to manage that. The rescue team never saw Ms Nilsson at the camp.'

'Excellent.' Ashraf looked at his watch. 'Have we finished?' He'd already been delayed for hours. He wanted to see how Tori and Oliver were settling in. Make sure she wasn't planning to get the next plane out of there.

Not that she'd succeed.

But it wasn't merely that concerning him. The look she'd sent him at the airport when he'd told her to go with Bram had revealed how much he'd asked of her. For a second she'd looked beseeching. The sight had stunned him as even her moment of panic on the plane hadn't.

Before today he'd seen Tori shocked, struggling to process the news that he was alive, and he'd seen her battling to hide terror during their kidnap. But her vulnerability in that split second when her gaze had clung had curdled his gut.

It had taken more determination than he'd imagined to watch her walk away before turning calmly to the officials awaiting him.

Ashraf had wanted to lash out at the politician whose judgemental gaze had rested so dismissively on Tori. Who'd inserted himself into the royal schedule solely, Ashraf knew, to make mischief. He'd wanted to turn his back on the high-level meeting that had been arranged in his absence.

But instead Ashraf had quashed the impulse to ignore his regal responsibility and go with Tori and Oliver—his family.

The word snagged the breath in his lungs.

Given his utterly dysfunctional family background, Ashraf had never dwelled on the idea of creating a family of his own. Now he had one. The realisation was arresting, satisfying and disturbing.

The sound of Bram clearing his throat jerked Ashraf's attention back. 'Yes? Is there something else?'

'Nothing.'

For second he could have sworn he saw amusement in his friend's eyes. But the next moment Bram was frowning at the royal schedule.

'We're finished for today, but tomorrow's timetable is packed. Suddenly half the Cabinet Ministers need to see you urgently.'

Ashraf lifted one eyebrow. 'I'm sure they do.' He shook his head, resisting the urge to massage those tight neck muscles again. 'If only they spent as much energy on public policy as they do trying to undermine me.'

'Actually, on that… It's too soon to tell, but you may have had a couple more wins. Two provincial governors have been in contact privately this week, full of enthusiasm about the results of your latest initiatives. They're hoping to meet you to discuss ideas they have for further implementation.' Bram paused. 'It could be that the tide is turning.'

Or it could be that you'll never be accepted, no matter how hard you work or how sound your policies. You're an outsider. You always have been. Nothing will change that.

The voice in Ashraf's head wasn't new. It had always been there, undercutting his early attempts to be a son his father could be proud of.

With the ease of long practice he ignored it. 'Let's hope.'

And he hoped, too, that he could win Tori over. She'd agreed to this visit but persuading her to stay, to accept his proposition, would take all his persuasive skills and more.

Tori hadn't answered his knock so he entered her suite, taking in the silence and lengthening shadows. A quick investigation revealed no sign of her or Oliver.

Ashraf frowned. Had she turned tail and left the palace? But that wasn't like Tori. Nevertheless he felt better seeing her clothes in the wardrobe.

He retraced his steps to the sitting room, then went out into the suite's private courtyard. A slow smile curved his lips and warmed his belly.

Tori lay on a sun lounger set in dappled shade beside the long pool. A portable cot where Oliver dozed was positioned beside her.

Heat thwacked Ashraf's chest as he looked at his tiny son. And as for Tori...

His gaze trailed over her silver gilt hair, enticingly loose across her narrow shoulders. Over the open shirt and slinky scarlet bikini that revealed full breasts and a narrow waist. Down lissom bare legs.

His groin stirred as desire smoked across his skin. He wanted Victoria Nilsson. Wanted her naked and eager. Wanted so much more. Everything he discovered about this woman attracted him. Plus, he wanted all that maternal love for his son.

Ashraf drew a deep breath, relieved at the reason for these unusually intense feelings. The need to provide for his son. That explained his determination to have Tori permanently. Ashraf wanted the very best for his boy. That meant Oliver's mother to love and care for their son. As Ashraf's mother hadn't been around to love and care for him.

As if she sensed his scrutiny Tori's eyelids fluttered open. For a second Ashraf read pleasure in those forget-me-not-blue eyes. Pleasure and welcome. But only for a second.

Too soon she was scrambling to sit up, hauling her shirt closed with one hand, eyes wary.

'Relax.'

Ashraf sank onto a nearby chair, looking around the courtyard. He needed to concentrate on something other than Tori. He refused to betray the urgency that sang in his blood when she was near.

Yet even with his gaze elsewhere he was aware of her. The soft hitch of her breath, the creak of her chair as she moved, her sweet, tantalising scent.

He forced himself to focus on his surroundings. He

hadn't been in here before. The royal family's rooms were on the other side of the palace and he'd never investigated the guest apartments. Bram had chosen well. The courtyard was restful and private.

'Does the apartment suit you? If it's lacking anything…'

'Lacking?' Tori shook her head and that stunning hair spilled around her shoulders. 'It's beautiful. More than we need.'

Ashraf dragged his attention back to her face, to the frown lines between her brows. As if she was worried she'd been allocated something to which she wasn't entitled.

Didn't Tori realise how much more she'd be entitled to as his wife? Or was she really not concerned with wealth?

Another reminder that she wasn't like the women he'd known.

'I'm glad to see you resting. It's been a turbulent time for you.'

Ashraf congratulated himself on his tact. Far better than blurting out that she looked tired. How she'd managed those months alone with Oliver and starting a new, demanding job…

'Now, *there's* an understatement.'

A ghost of a smile curved her lips and Ashraf felt his tension lessen.

Once more he sensed a fragile understanding and acceptance between them. It was rare. He'd only experienced it before with his brother and Bram, the two men who really knew him and rather than just his reputation.

Deliberately Ashraf settled back and let his eyes rove the tranquil garden. Sweet blossom perfumed the air and from nearby came the chitter of a bird.

How long since he'd taken an evening off?

His gaze turned to the small table beside Tori. A newspaper lay there, and a book. He tilted his head to read the title.

'You're learning my language?' Satisfaction glowed. This was a good sign.

Tori made a deprecating gesture. 'Trying. A little. It seemed like a good idea.'

'It's an excellent idea.' He beamed and watched her eyes widen. 'But you don't need to use a book. I'll arrange a tutor.'

Instead of thanking him, she frowned. 'That's not necessary. I'm only here on a visit.'

So much for seeing this as an indication that she'd decided to stay. Ashraf schooled his features not to reveal emotion, but that didn't stop the bite of disappointment.

'You can't *really* expect marriage, Ashraf,' she said when he didn't respond.

Her voice was low but he heard the echo of the arguments she'd put up before. Arguments she thought were reasonable but which meant nothing in the face of his all-consuming need to protect his child.

Impatience grated. How did he make her understand? Make her see the damage that threatened little Oliver if they didn't work together to protect him?

Ashraf knew Tori's relationship with her father wasn't close now, but surely she'd grown up with a mother and father, a sense of belonging. She'd been nurtured and, he guessed, loved.

Oliver would survive with the love of both his parents even if those parents weren't together. Yet that wasn't enough for Ashraf. Not when he knew first-hand the isolation of being different. The poisonous rumours. The continual battle to be accepted.

Ashraf would do anything to ensure his son didn't face that. He didn't want Oliver merely to survive. He wanted him to thrive.

Ashraf expelled a slow breath, realising there was only one way to convince Tori. He'd planned to seduce her into agreement. But, while that might help, Tori was a woman who thought things through. Who weighed up options and responsibilities. Sexual pleasure wouldn't be enough. She needed concrete reasons.

The thought of baring those reasons filled him with cold nausea. Even with Bram and Karim the past was a territory he didn't visit.

'Family is very important,' he began.

'Of course. But Oliver can have that without us marrying.'

'Not the sort of family he'll need.'

'Sorry?'

'Za'daq is a modern country but it still has traditional roots. Traditional values.'

'You're saying we should marry because you're worried about what people will *think*?' Her mouth tightened. 'You believe public opinion is worth an unhappy marriage?'

'You assume it will be unhappy?'

Tori spread her hands. 'We don't know each other. We probably don't have anything in common—'

'We have Oliver.' That made her pause. 'And we have more too. Respect.' Ashraf held her eyes. 'Liking. Attraction.'

White-hot desire was a better description, but he

sensed she'd baulk at such straight talking. He'd seen her nervous reaction to the craving they both felt.

'That's not enough.'

'You want romantic love?' He searched her face, watching her gaze skitter away.

'It's usually the basis of marriage.'

'In your country, but not mine. Here love often comes with time, with respect, with liking and shared experience. All of which we have.'

'We shared one night of captivity!'

'An intense experience. You can't deny the connection between us is strong because of it. Far stronger than if we'd met on an online site and begun dating.'

Tori pursed her lips but said nothing.

'We have what it takes to make a good marriage. For Oliver's sake we need to try.'

Ashraf paused but she refused to admit his point. He ignored the churning in his belly and plunged on.

'I want our son to have what I didn't. Two parents who care for him. Who are there for him every day.' He watched her brow knot. 'Every child deserves a supportive environment. Without that life can be tough.' His lips curled as a sour tang filled his mouth. 'I don't want that for Oliver.'

'I didn't know your childhood was difficult.' There was curiosity and sympathy in Tori's look, but instead of pressing for details she went on. 'But I don't see how that applies to Oliver.'

Ashraf shook his head. 'I want Oliver to have the best in every way. I can declare him legitimate, and that will give him legal status, but I want him to be part of a *real* family. To give meaning to the bare legality and make it something more.' He paused and turned to look at the innocent child who, he knew, would suffer if Ashraf wasn't careful.

Suddenly his lungs ached, pain searing deep.

'I want him protected from scorn and prejudice.' He took another slow breath that still didn't fill his chest. 'Above all I don't want him to believe, for a moment, that I'm not committed to him or don't want him here. I won't have him growing up in the shadows, unsure where he fits.'

Tori's arguments stilled on her tongue as she read the lines of tension wrapping around Ashraf's mouth and pleating his forehead. An icy wave washed over her, despite the balmy evening.

Here was something she didn't understand. Something important. Ashraf wasn't posturing. Whatever the problem was, it was deep-seated. She felt the ache of it just watching his still frame as he stared at Oliver.

'What do you mean, growing up in the shadows?'

Ashraf turned and for the first time she could recall, his dark eyes looked utterly bleak. But only for a moment. Just as she was registering what looked like anguish, his expression became unreadable.

He lifted wide shoulders and spread his hands. 'I wasn't meant to be Sheikh, you know.'

Slowly Tori nodded. 'You said your older brother was supposed to inherit. Is this something to do with him?

'*No.*' The word was emphatic. 'Karim's reasons for rejecting the throne are his own and private.' He paused as if to make sure she got the 'no trespassing' message.

Tori got it, all right, but that didn't stifle her curiosity. She watched as Ashraf swung his legs off the lounger to sit facing her, elbows on his thighs. The stance emphasised the power in his athletic frame and awareness fluttered through her, making her hurry into speech.

'So you weren't first in line to the throne… What's that saying? Having an heir and a spare lined up?'

Ashraf's huff of laughter was humourless. 'Good in theory, but I was never the spare—not as far as my father was concerned. He hated me because I wasn't his.'

'Not his?' Astonishment gripped her.

'My mother left him for another man when I was tiny. The official story in Za'daq is that she died. My father couldn't bear the thought of the public knowing the truth. In those days the press was carefully controlled. Nothing went public that would offend the Sheikh.'

Tori shook her head, still grappling with the first part of what he'd said. 'She left to be with another man? The man who'd fathered you? Yet she didn't take you?'

She couldn't imagine leaving her baby behind.

'She knew the Sheikh wouldn't denounce me as illegitimate because his pride wouldn't permit a public scandal. She was right. Publicly, he didn't.'

Ashraf's expression, as hard as cast bronze, confirmed that in private things had been different.

'Surely she could have taken you?'

'You didn't know his pride.' Ashraf shook his head. 'Once he'd acknowledged me as his son he'd never release me. Anyway, she probably thought I'd be better off here. Her lover wasn't wealthy.'

Tori stared, her mind racing. 'You never *asked* her why she left you behind?'

His mouth tightened. 'I didn't get a chance. She died of complications from influenza when I was a child. I only discovered that later—when I set out to locate her.'

Tori sank back, stunned. Ashraf an unloved child…
abandoned by his mother and left to the mercy of a
proud, arrogant man for whom he was a reminder of
his wife's desertion. Her skin crawled.

'I never had what you'd call a family life.'

Ashraf's voice was uninflected. He might have been
talking about the weather.

'Except for my brother, Karim, no one cared about
me.'

He drew a breath that made his chest rise, then
turned to lock his gaze with hers.

'My father never told anyone about my parentage
but he made his disapproval clear to me in every possible way. There was no warmth or encouragement.
He constantly found fault and his attitude rubbed off.
The courtiers, all the people who mattered in Za'daq,
took their cue from him. Everyone viewed me as use-
less, shallow, lacking the virtues my brother possessed.
Whispers and innuendo followed me no matter how
hard I tried.'

'So you acted up?'

She thought of those press reports about the Playboy
Prince, spending his time flitting between scandalous
parties and shockingly dangerous sports. Because he'd
had nothing better to do with his time? Or because he
too had believed he had nothing better to offer?

Tori's hand went to her throat. It was hard to imagine Ashraf, of all people, so vulnerable.

His mouth twisted. 'As a kid I tried hard to please
my father. But nothing was good enough. Later…' He
shrugged. 'Later it seemed a fine revenge to make him
squirm a little by living down to the reputation he'd
built for me.'

She didn't know what to say. Finally she asked, 'Did you ever meet your real father?'

Ashraf's expression had been wry before, his features taut. Now, though, it was as if an iron shutter slammed down, blocking out even the cynical amusement that had gleamed in that half-smile a moment before.

'That's the ultimate irony. When the old Sheikh was taken ill he needed a bone marrow donor. Even though he was so sick he still couldn't bring himself to countermand the suggestion that I get tested for compatibility. That's when we discovered I *was* his son after all. He'd spent years despising me on the basis of unfounded suspicion. Just because he'd found an old letter that predated my birth, sent to my mother by the man she later ran off with. He assumed—wrongly—that she'd slept with him and conceived me as a result.'

'Oh, Ashraf.'

She sat up, instinctively covering his clasped hands with one of hers. It was like touching warm but unforgiving steel. All that hate. All that distance between father and son for nothing but pride.

One of those large hands moved and covered hers. Eyes dark as a stormy night captured hers.

'I want Oliver to have what I never did. A family. Parents together in one place, loving him, caring for him—'

He broke off and Tori wondered with a wobble of distress if Ashraf's throat had closed as convulsively as hers had. She swallowed, trying to dislodge the choking knot of emotion blocking her larynx as she imagined his childhood.

'I don't give a damn what people think of me. But I

don't want him subjected to prejudice because he's not in my life full-time. Because he's not seen to belong.'

Her gaze slewed to their precious boy, who'd woken and was now staring at them with lustrous eyes so like Ashraf's that her chest squeezed.

'He *does* belong. He's ours.'

But as she spoke Tori's heart sank. Ashraf was right. Oliver could be legitimised, but to some his birth out of wedlock would for ever leave a taint of scandal.

'Whether he's in Australia or Za'daq he'll attract public interest. It's inevitable. I want to do everything to protect him from the negatives of that. I want to support him. I want him to feel safe and secure, proud of who he is. Sure right from the start that we're united and on his side.'

Ashraf's voice rang with sincerity. Tori wanted that too. She could understand Ashraf's reasoning now, and her heart ached for the boy he'd been, a victim of circumstances beyond his control, abandoned by both parents.

Part of her wanted to nod and say of course she'd do anything for her son. Yet even as she opened her mouth her own survival instinct kicked in. Everything rebelled at the thought of marrying for appearances' sake.

Flashes of memory filled her brain. Of her parents' marriage where whatever tenderness there might once have been had died. All that had remained was a sham, a pretence of a happy family constructed to salvage pride and win votes.

Tori had vowed never to have a marriage like that. Since childhood she'd known she wanted more. She'd promised herself she'd never settle for anything less than love.

'I...' She met Ashraf's gaze and her throat dried. She was torn between determination to do what was best for Oliver and fear that she'd become like her mother, living an unhappy half-life. 'I need time.'

After what seemed like a full minute he nodded. 'Of course. I understand.'

But that wasn't what his eyes said, or the pressure of his hand on hers. He was a determined man. A king. How far would his patience stretch?

CHAPTER EIGHT

FOUR DAYS LATER Tori knew Ashraf's patience was far stronger than hers.

Heat climbed her cheeks as she realised she almost *wanted* him to break the impasse between them. She lived on tenterhooks, feeling the tension screwing tighter with each hour.

Despite her reservations about marriage, Tori couldn't switch off her intense response to Ashraf's magnetism. The yearning for his touch, his tenderness, his body, just wouldn't fade. She remembered being in his arms, lost in a sensual abandon so profound the world had fallen away. The memories were fresher than ever and more tempting.

Late each day he came to her rooms to share a meal and spend time with Oliver. From that they'd begun to develop a new type of intimacy which was simultaneously challenging and precious.

Despite the unanswered question hanging over them, those hours were relaxing and companionable. Ashraf never mentioned marriage. He was an easy, amusing companion, sharing anecdotes and asking about her day, fascinated by what she and Oliver had done.

Nor did he shy from answering her questions. His

frankness intrigued her, especially when she discovered areas of common ground or subjects in which their differing views led to stimulating debate.

Debate, not argument.

Unlike her father, Ashraf never tried to browbeat her into accepting his views.

It was her favourite time of the day. A time she recalled late at night, long after Ashraf had left and she'd retired to her lonely bed.

Tori shivered and stared absently at the tiny shop's display of bright fabrics. She lifted the filigreed glass of tea to her lips. The scalding liquid warmed her and might even explain the flush she felt in her cheeks.

What she recalled most often, and in excruciating detail, was how Ashraf, after kissing Oliver on the brow, always took her hand and pressed a lingering kiss there as he said goodnight. His eyes shone like polished onyx and he held her hand so long she was sure he must feel the throb of her pulse racing out of control.

Every night she wondered if *this* would be the moment he'd break his self-imposed distance and pull her close, giving in to the ever-present spark of desire between them.

And every night, just as she decided she couldn't stand the suspense or the longing any more, he'd say goodnight and leave her alone in her sumptuous apartment.

'I won't be much longer, Tori. I promise.'

Azia's voice interrupted her thoughts. Tori looked towards the crimson curtain that hid the small shop's changing room and smiled.

'Take your time. I'm enjoying all these fabulous silks. It's like being in Aladdin's cave.' She nodded to the shop owner, who beamed and pulled down a bolt of sea-green silk threaded with silver before taking it to Azia.

It was a treat to be on a girls' shopping expedition with Bram's wife, while a nanny looked after Azia's little daughter and Oliver. Two days ago, when Bram had introduced her to his wife, Tori had been reluctant to accept Azia's invitation to coffee in the city. She knew all about duty visits, having done her share while supporting her father.

But Azia's smile had been warm and Tori had longed to get away from the palace's gilded luxury. She loved her apartment, with its pretty courtyard and pool, but she didn't know her way around the massive building and didn't feel comfortable wandering through it.

To her surprise, their coffee date had been fun and Tori had laughed more than she had in ages. Azia had an irreverent sense of humour and a kind heart. The next day they went to lunch and visited an exhibition of exquisite beadwork by an upcoming designer.

Today they were at the silk shops in the bazaar, where Azia was determined to find fabric for a special outfit.

'How about this?' The curtains swished back to reveal Tori's new friend draped in green and silver.

Tori tilted her head. 'It's very beautiful…'

'But…? Come on, tell me.'

'Personally, I loved that bright lime-green. This one is pretty, but that bright pop of colour really complemented your colouring.'

Azia laughed, but her expression was uncertain. 'I liked that one too but it might be a bit too bright.'

'Too bright?' Tori frowned. 'Why shouldn't you wear bright colours? You look fantastic in them.'

Her friend shrugged. 'It's for a royal event and…' She glanced at the shop owner, who took the hint and moved towards the front of the shop, giving them some privacy.

Azia shrugged. 'I don't really fit in there. I'm not high-born and nor is Bram. Last time I went to a reception I overheard comments—' She shook her head. 'It doesn't matter. I just want to fit in.'

Her words echoed Ashraf's, jolting Tori's composure. Who *were* these people who busied themselves making others feel out of place? What gave them the right to judge? Because they were rich or born into powerful families?

Tori knew about the flaws hidden in many powerful and 'perfect' families.

'Which colour makes you happy?'

'The lime,' Azia answered instantly.

'Then buy the lime. You look beautiful in it.'

Azia wavered, then nodded. 'You're right. I will. Thank you.'

With a rattle of curtain rings she stepped back into the changing cubicle, leaving Tori alone with her thoughts. Inevitably they returned to Ashraf. He'd spoken of not being accepted. How had that moulded him into the man he was? He wasn't uncertain or insecure. In fact he was one of the most determined people she knew.

But what if Oliver wasn't strong enough to endure the censure of others so easily? Her spirits plunged. Was she selfish, refusing to marry Ashraf and give Oliver a conventional family? Not all conventional families were like hers, where only one parent had loved and supported her.

Her father had been too wrapped up in his career to care for anyone but himself. He'd married Tori's mother because she came from a family with money and political influence. Tori had always thought if she married it would be to someone who wanted *her*, not what she represented.

She sighed and put down her tea. At least she and her mother had been close. How Tori wished she were here now, to talk over this enormous decision.

For the first time she understood why her mother had stayed with her father. For the security he offered while she raised Tori. A woman would put up with a lot for her child.

Not that Ashraf would be a hands-off father, like her dad. On the contrary, he'd be very hands-on—

'You look flushed.' Azia emerged with a bolt of bright silk under her arm. 'I'm sorry, I shouldn't have taken so long.' She paused. 'Do you already have something for the reception or should we look now?'

'I'm not going.' Tori got up from the visitor's chair.

'You're not? But...' Azia looked confused. 'It's a very special event, hosted by the Sheikh himself. You'd enjoy it. There's music and traditional dancing as well as a spectacular feast.'

Tori shrugged, suppressing a pang of regret. It did sound interesting. 'I don't have an invitation.'

Azia's brow knotted. 'That's impossible. Bram wouldn't forget your invitation. He *never* forgets—' She broke off as the shop owner bustled forward to complete the sale.

Hours later, as the sun paused above the horizon, making the sky ribbons of scarlet and tangerine, Tori entered her private courtyard. It was beautiful, with its delicate marble arches and fragrant garden.

Her gaze strayed to the long green-tiled pool. Ashraf had been delayed. She had time to swim before he arrived. She liked swimming, but hadn't done much since Oliver's birth—partly from lack of time and partly because of babysitting costs. This was a wonderful luxury.

Tori was grateful to Ashraf. If nothing else, she welcomed this break from solo parenting. She felt better for more sleep and proper exercise. Nor did she miss the early starts, getting herself and Oliver ready each day, or dealing with Steve Bates and office politics. Her job was good, but not the workplace.

She reached the end of the pool and turned, the rhythmic strokes inviting her mind to drift to the upcoming royal reception.

It was curious that Ashraf hadn't mentioned it. According to Azia, there'd be hundreds of guests. But not Tori. Silly to feel left out. She didn't *want* to attend stuffy official events. She'd done enough of that for her father.

Except this didn't sound stuffy. Invitees would enjoy displays by acrobats, swordsmen, riders and archers, including a feat where galloping horsemen shot flaming arrows into impossibly tiny targets.

Strange… Wouldn't Ashraf see this as a chance to showcase his culture? To introduce her to his friends? Instead he kept her secluded like a woman in an old-fashioned harem.

Or an embarrassment he didn't want anyone to discover.

The thought slammed into her and she swallowed

water. An embarrassment? Was that how he saw her and Oliver?

Tori flicked her hair from her eyes and gasped in a lungful of air. No, Ashraf wasn't like that.

Except the day they'd arrived he'd spoken to her like a casual acquaintance, not a lover. Anyone watching wouldn't guess they'd been intimate. At the time she'd been grateful to him for helping her to save face before strangers. But what if he had another reason?

He'd sent her off immediately, not even introducing her to the man who'd met them. Plus he hadn't accompanied her to the palace as she'd expected.

Despite refusing him, you still want his attention, don't you? You want to be with him. Want him to want you.

The truth taunted her and she shied away from it.

Ashraf—hiding her?

She recalled that first day. The limo avoiding the palace's main entrance to use the back gate. Bram hurrying her inside—to avoid curious eyes? Bram telling her that this apartment was at the rear of the palace and quiet. She'd thought that considerate, but maybe it was because she and Oliver were an embarrassment.

It fitted with what Ashraf had said about prejudice. And with what Azia had hinted.

Bile was sour on Tori's tongue as she swam to the poolside and levered herself out. She shivered and turned to grab her towel—only to see it being held out for her.

'Ashraf!'

Tori's voice was harsh, as if he was the last person she'd expected. No, it was more than that. She didn't sound surprised as much as put out. As if she didn't *wish* to see him.

Impatience stirred. And a trickle of annoyance. He'd looked forward to the end of an interminable yet necessary meeting so he could enjoy a few hours with her. Didn't he deserve a warmer welcome?

Tori should be used to his presence. Yet the pool's underwater lights and the antique lanterns around the colonnaded courtyard revealed a face set in severe lines. And a body as arousing as ever.

Usually she smiled when he appeared, though it took her a while to relax fully. Ashraf had told himself that she needed time to adjust. But part of him—the part that had always taken for granted his ability to attract any woman he wanted—felt it like an insult.

He'd been patient. Beyond patient. He'd ignored his own needs to put hers and Oliver's first.

Since his accession he'd put the needs of his people and his country before his own and he didn't regret a second of it. But with Tori his altruism faltered when he looked into her wide blue eyes and felt the tug of desire in his loins. And when she stood before him in a skimpy scarlet bikini he had to pretend not to notice her sumptuous sexiness.

'Sorry I'm late.' The day had been difficult and he'd looked forward to her company. Clearly she didn't feel the same. 'I've already checked on Oliver. He's fast asleep.'

Tori took the towel and hurriedly wound it round her body. Annoyance jagged him again. Didn't she trust him? He had treated her as his honoured guest. He'd put no pressure on her for intimacy. He'd been scrupulous about giving her time and space to consider the arguments in favour of marriage.

For a man used to quick decisions and immediate follow-through his restraint had been remarkable. Yet did she appreciate it?

His mouth tightened. 'Is something wrong?'

She tucked in the end of the towel firmly, as if daring it to slip.

Ashraf forced down his irritation. It would achieve nothing. 'You're frowning.'

'Am I? No, nothing's wrong.'

One stubborn woman resisted him. One woman whose fears he understood, which was why he'd held back rather than forcing the issue between them.

'Shall we go in? Supper has been laid out inside.' Hunger for food was one appetite he *could* satisfy.

'Not yet.'

Tori's tone was over-loud, her words quick. Her jaw had firmed, the way it did when she argued and when she'd masked her fear during their abduction.

Ashraf's frustration dissipated. How could he blame her for being cautious? She was facing such major changes.

'I have a question,' she said.

Maybe it was about what her life would be like in Za'daq. Pleased, Ashraf nodded. 'Go on.'

Tori crossed her arms over her chest and fire kindled in her eyes. 'Are you *ashamed* of me and Oliver?'

'Ashamed?' The idea was outrageous.

'Or just a little embarrassed?'

Tori's expression morphed into a searing disapproval that would have done his father proud. Even with her moonlight-pale hair dripping rivulets down her shoulders and chest she looked strong, compelling. And angry.

She wasn't the only one. 'Where did you get such an idea?'

'You're not answering the question.'

Her hands went to her hips, pulling the towel down to reveal more of her breasts. Ashraf dragged his attention back to her face and her perplexing words.

'That's ridiculous. Who suggested that?' If one of his political enemies had been bothering Tori he'd—

'No one. I'm able to think for myself.'

Ashraf frowned. 'But you *can't* think that.'

Surely his actions showed that he respected her? He'd gone out of his way to ease her into this new world. It was true he'd rushed her back to Za'daq because he couldn't afford more time out of the country right now, and because instinct had demanded he keep her and his son close. But otherwise he'd been the acme of consideration.

'You haven't answered me.'

That rounded chin tilted and Ashraf felt an urge to angle it even higher, so he could slam his mouth down on hers. He'd stop her insults and take out his frustrations as he ravished her mouth, then moved on to ravishing her body.

'I'm neither ashamed nor embarrassed about you and Oliver.' He held her haughty stare with one of his own and watched her eyebrows twitch in confusion. 'What gave you such an idea?'

Tori held herself stiffly. She clearly didn't believe him.

The realisation ground through him like glass grating beneath his heel. Except he felt it inside—as if his windpipe and belly were lined with shards. No one, not even those vultures waiting for him to fail as Sheikh, had ever accused him of untruth. Ashraf's hackles rose.

'It's the way we live here in the palace…alone, not mixing with other people.'

'I understood that you and Azia had been out together for the last three days?'

The fire in Tori's eyes flickered. She hadn't expected him to know about that. He breathed deep, biting back the impulse to tell her it had been *his* suggestion that Bram's wife visit her.

'Yes, we have. But if it weren't for her Oliver and I would be isolated here. Except for your visits late in the day.'

Ashraf stared. In other words, his presence counted for nothing. The hours he carved out of his packed schedule weren't appreciated. *He* wasn't appreciated.

Fleetingly Ashraf felt something dark and hurtful—a whispered memory of all those times when he'd tried to please his father and failed. But that boy was long gone. Ashraf had moulded himself into a man who would *never* be needy.

'Is that all?'

She must have heard a trace of suppressed anger in his tone for her hands slipped from her waist and she wrapped her arms around herself. Yet still she held his gaze.

'No. There are other things. The way we were hurried off from the airport without being introduced to anyone except Bram. Even when we got here Bram hurried us inside so fast that I wonder if he was worried we'd be seen. We always use the back entrance, and this apartment is at the rear of the palace. Is it because you don't want anyone knowing about us?'

Ashraf opened his mouth to respond but she hurried on.

'You spoke about marrying because of people's prejudice when your father believed you were illegitimate. You're worried about what other people think. And...' she sucked in a quick breath '...I'm obviously not good enough to attend your big celebration next week.'

He stared down into her flushed face, torn between fury at the insult and regret that Tori should believe that for a second. His hands clenched so tight the blood was restricted and his fingers tingled. He flexed them and shoved them in his pockets.

'First, Bram probably hurried you inside because he was worried about you coping with the heat—especially when you were tired from a long journey. Second, I didn't introduce you to the man who met our plane because his sole purpose in being there was to find out about you so he could make trouble. He's the Minister for the Interior, one of my father's oldest cronies, and he's devoted to the idea of unseating me from the throne. Call me prejudiced, but I didn't want him to be the first Za'daqi you met.'

Ashraf rocked back on his feet, forcing further explanations through clenched teeth.

'As for you being at the rear of the palace—that *was* intentional. Because I believed you needed rest. And I thought you'd appreciate some peace while you acclimatised and thought through your options for the future.'

So much for her appreciating his efforts on her behalf!

'You haven't been isolated. I moved out of the royal

suite to be near you and Oliver.' He nodded to the windows on the side of the courtyard adjoining her rooms. 'I've spent every night since you arrived right next door. If you care to check, there's a concealed door between the suites. The staff have instructions to wake me if you call for assistance in the night.'

'I...I had no idea!' Tori's eyes rounded. 'Why didn't you say?'

'Foolishly, I thought you might feel pressured. As if I were encroaching by wanting to help out if Oliver had teething pains.'

Strange how he missed those night-time sessions, pacing the floor with a fractious baby. But holding his son in his arms, knowing he was building a bond that would last a lifetime, had stirred new and incredibly strong emotions.

Those hours in Tori's home, watching her feed Oliver, doing what he could to ease the burden, had held an intimacy and significance against which everything else paled. Even his royal responsibilities couldn't eclipse that.

Tori unwrapped her arms and the towel slid off, revealing her bikini-clad body, but she didn't notice. She stared as if she'd never seen him before.

'And I haven't introduced you to people at court yet because I respect your wish for privacy. You insisted this was a private visit, to test the waters. You *know*—' his voice ground low '—that I want to introduce you as my future bride.'

Ashraf's lungs tightened again at all her unjust accusations.

'I am not and never will be ashamed of either you or our son.' He paused, giving her time to absorb that.

'Yes, I've faced prejudice because of my father's attitude. No, I don't want Oliver to suffer anything like that. But I'm not *afraid* of public opinion.' He barely restrained his bitter laughter. 'I've lived with scandal so long I'm used to it. Most of the time it's in the minds of others rather than based on something I've actually done.'

Deliberately he moved into her personal space, leaning so close that her evocative scent blurred his senses.

'I want to marry you to give Oliver the best start in life. Not because I'm scared of tittle-tattle.'

'Ashraf, I—'

'And you haven't received a written invitation to the reception because I wanted to invite you myself. It's a perfect chance for you to see something of my culture, meet people and enjoy yourself. I wanted to give you time to rest and acclimatise before mentioning it.'

He'd been sure his painfully patient approach would bear fruit. That Tori would see the wisdom of his proposal and accept. It appeared patience wasn't working.

Tori blinked up at him. Finally she cleared her throat, moistening her lips in an unconsciously provocative movement that, to Ashraf's annoyance, shot a bolt of lust through him.

Even angry, he wanted this woman. Even after she'd questioned his honour and tested his patience to the limit.

Eyes the colour of a soft spring sky met his. 'I'm sorry, Ashraf. I got it completely wrong.'

'You did.'

Indignation still ran like a living current under his skin, heating his blood. This woman drove him crazy. She fought him over things that were, in his opinion, patently obvious, yet at other times was so reasonable it surprised him. Like accepting his need to see Oliver immediately and to be involved in his life.

And it wasn't just her contrary reasoning that exasperated him. Her ability to ignore the rampant attraction between them was unprecedented and provoking. While *he*, damn it, was distracted by the sight of those lush breasts rising and falling beneath the skimpy triangles of fabric. And the gleaming abundance of slick, pale skin.

'I should be thanking you, not accusing you.'

She lifted her hand to his sleeve. Ashraf stilled. Her touch was light, barely there, yet he felt it acutely.

'It's no excuse but, nice as it is to relax, I feel dislocated, cut off from work and home. I've overreacted. Can you forgive me?'

A huff of laughter escaped Ashraf. 'I don't suppose you feel chastened enough to marry me?'

Her eyes widened, as if he'd suggested something shockingly debauched instead of honouring her with a proposal that would make her a queen and the envy of half the women in Za'daq.

The anger that her apology had quenched spiked anew. Impatience surged.

'Is that a no?'

He turned his hand, capturing hers. His fingers encircled her wrist and he detected the wild pulse hammering there. Was she really so timid? Or was that arousal?

Ashraf was tired of tiptoeing around Tori's doubts. Tired of waiting. Tired of holding back.

'In that case, this will have to do.'

He tugged her close and she fell flush against him,

her breasts to his torso, her other palm on his chest. To steady herself or to push him away?

Ashraf didn't wait to find out. In the same instant he roped his other arm around her slick body, lowered his head and kissed her full on the lips.

CHAPTER NINE

TORI SAW THOSE mesmerising eyes glitter and knew a moment of sharp, shocking anticipation.

Not dismay. Not even a second of doubt. Just anticipation.

It thrilled through her like an electric current, making all the fine hairs on her body lift and her breath seize. Then Ashraf's mouth was on hers, hard and demanding rather than coaxing.

She didn't need coaxing. Tori was primed and ready for his kiss. Had been from the moment he'd walked back into her life and some primitive part of her had hummed with excitement and want.

She wanted him so badly.

Relief was profound as she finally gave in to what she'd secretly craved. In this moment she didn't need to reason, or argue, or try to unknot the tangle of her mixed emotions. All she needed to do was feel.

She loved the taste of him, the heat and extraordinary *maleness* of him, hard and unrelenting. From that first instant there'd been no coercion. Just a demand that she was eager to meet. It had always been like this with him.

Her lips softened beneath his, inviting him in, all but begging him for more. He took up her offer and a shudder racked her as his tongue plunged deep, swirling against hers, exploring with a thoroughness that mixed determination and expertise. It was like tumbling through bright starlight, ceding control to this man whom she knew would never let her fall.

Ashraf scooped her closer, his hard frame solid muscle against her wet body. Tori clung tight, one hand clutching his robe, the other slipping from his grasp to slide up the back of his neck.

She heard a muffled grunt of approval as her fingers channelled through thick hair to splay possessively over the back of his head.

Her tongue danced with his, hunger cresting as she went up on her toes, trying to meld herself to him. His taste, his scent, his mouth were achingly familiar, as if it was just a few days since they'd made love.

Had they kissed like this in the desert? Surely not. Then they'd been strangers. Ashraf didn't feel like a stranger now. Remarkable to think they'd been together such a short time, for it seemed they knew each other at some deep level beyond words. He was the man who filled her thoughts and dreams. Who had done so since that night together. He was the one man who'd woken her dormant libido after the rigours and exhaustion of pregnancy and motherhood.

The one man she needed as she'd never before needed anyone.

The realisation made her freeze in his embrace.

Instantly he lifted his head, eyes glinting like black gems as they searched her face.

Tori heard the stertorous rasp of heavy breathing, felt her lungs heave and the push of his chest against her breasts as he too hauled in oxygen. Reaction jud-

dered down her backbone and quivered across her skin.
Being so close to him, touching him, undid her carefully cultivated caution. It allowed something wild inside her to take hold.

The air was smoky with desire, thick and scented
with arousal. Yet the unspoken question was clear in
Ashraf's expression. Did she want to stop?

She was bent back over his arm, plastered to him,
so she felt the uneven catch of his breathing and his
waiting stillness. They were on the brink of far more
than a kiss. It was there in the taut awareness singing
between them. But even now Ashraf would release her
if she wanted.

Emotion swelled. As strong as the desire emblazoned
in her bones. Tenderness for this man who put her needs
before his own. It struck her how remarkable that was,
given that Ashraf literally had all the power in this
kingdom of his.

Now her earlier doubts about him seemed absurd.
She'd never met anyone with such innate integrity.

Tori shivered at the enormity of her feelings. Yet still
she shied away from investigating them too closely.

Ashraf straightened and pulled away. He'd misread
her.

'No!' She fastened both hands on his shoulders, fingers digging into fine cotton, pads of muscle and beneath that implacable bone. 'Don't.'

'Don't kiss you or—?'

'Don't stop.'

Yet instead of closing the gap Ashraf surveyed her
as if he felt none of her urgency. Only the flare of his
nostrils betrayed that he'd been affected too.

'So there's at least one thing about me you approve of.'

He wanted to *talk*? Frustration surged—and suspicion. 'Are you fishing for compliments?'

She spied a flicker of movement at the corner of his mouth and a tingle of delight teased her.

'No. But I'll take any you want to throw my way.' His lips firmed. 'You're not a woman easily swept off her feet, Victoria Miranda Nilsson.'

Tori shook her head, a snort of bitter laughter escaping. 'Really? Don't forget I'm the woman who had sex with a stranger in a prison cell after just a couple of hours' acquaintance.'

She shivered, remembering her father's disgust even at the airbrushed version she'd recounted to him.

In the desert what she and Ashraf had done had felt utterly right—a blessing rather than anything else. But after her father's talk of hushing up a dirty secret and Ashraf's talk of illegitimacy—

'And I'm the man who found solace and hope in sharing my body with a stranger in that same prison cell.' Firm fingers cupped her chin, easing it up. 'You're not ashamed of us, are you?' He didn't wait for her answer. 'I'm not. You gave me a precious gift that night. Not just your body but your kindness, your passion and strength. Believe me…' his mouth rucked up in a wry smile '…to a man on Death Row they were a gift from Heaven.'

His words sank deep, warming her. Despite her determination not to relive the past, sometimes she couldn't quite believe she'd had sex with a man she didn't know. A wounded stranger she should have been nursing instead of seducing.

Yet memories of that night held magic as well as trauma.

Tori surveyed him intently. 'You're not on Death Row now.'

Every sense told her he shared the passion she felt. But could she trust her instincts? Was it possible that Ashraf's kiss had been motivated by pique at her questions and her refusal to accept marriage?

Her uncertainty surprised her. Surely the attraction between them was self-evident? Yet adrift from the world she knew, plonked into a fairy-tale palace with a handsome, powerful prince and experiencing an ardour she'd only known once before, it was easy to feel this wasn't real.

Maybe it was wishful thinking.

Her experience of sex was pretty limited. She might work in an industry dominated by men, but that just meant she'd got into the habit of shutting down attempts to engage her interest. Having a relationship with a co-worker was a complication she didn't need.

At her lower back one large hand splayed wide then pulled her close. Closer. Till she felt his arousal. A hot shiver raced through her and internal muscles warmed and softened.

'No.' His voice was rich and low, eddying deep within her. 'And you're not in prison here. You understand that, don't you? You're free to make your own choices.'

Ashraf regarded her steadily. She nodded. The claustrophobia she'd felt in this beautiful building was of her own making. Everyone here had been friendly and helpful. *She'd* been the one imagining she was confined to this part of the citadel. She'd found it easier to stay cloistered in this gorgeous apartment than to learn more about Ashraf's home.

Was she intimidated by his royal status, or by the fact she was being forced to share Oliver?

If Bram hadn't introduced her to Azia she'd probably never even have left this courtyard apartment. She'd have blamed it on tiredness. Or the need to protect her son from possible prejudice. When had she become so timid?

'And so...?'

His hands went to her hips. Tori loved his touch. Pleasure shimmered through her.

She tilted her head. 'And so...?' She refused to admit she'd lost the thread of the conversation.

The gleam in Ashraf's eyes told her he'd guessed, but for once she didn't mind that he found her easy to read.

'And so what would you like now? You're my honoured guest. It's my responsibility to see that your wishes are met.'

'My wish is your command?' Tori couldn't prevent the laugh bursting from her lips. It sounded like an *Arabian Nights* fantasy. Yet Ashraf's hard hands on her bare flesh turned her thoughts away from storybooks into an earthier direction.

'Something like that,' he murmured.

This time there was gravel mixed with the thick treacle of his voice. Tori shivered as it scraped her nerve-endings, drawing shuddery awareness in its wake. This, she realised, was the mesmerising voice of a man with the sexual experience of a playboy and the single-minded determination of the warrior Prince she'd come to know.

Was it any wonder her defences lay in splinters?

What was she defending herself against?

Ash...Ashraf...sought only what she longed to give.

Tori slipped her hands down over his cream robe. Her palms lingered on the swell of defined pectoral muscles and her belly clenched. Ever since that night she'd found him half-naked, cradling Oliver in those strong arms…

'There must be something you want.' His grip on her hips firmed and his warm breath trailed across her brow.

She nodded and licked dry lips. Then sucked in a fortifying breath as she saw the flare in his eyes. That look sent need quaking through her. She'd spent ages grieving this man's death and now he was here, so very alive. Contrary to what she'd told herself, absence hadn't exaggerated her reaction to him.

'I want you, Ash.'

It really was that simple.

Just as well that he held her, for his sudden smile undid her at the knees. She swayed and clutched his shoulders, her pulse sprinting at the sheer glory that was Ashraf's smile.

He leaned so close that Tori thought he was going to kiss her, but he stopped a tantalising breath away.

'Your wish…' his words caressed her face '…is my command.'

Then he swept her up in his arms as easily as if she weighed no more than Oliver. He made her feel small, something she'd never experienced before, being on the tall side of average. And he made her feel treasured which, she realised in a flash of revelation, no man except Ash, her desert lover, had made her feel.

Tori wrapped her hands around his neck and smiled. 'You do that very well. I think you've had practice.'

It was a sign of her infatuation that she didn't care.

He might have been a love-them-and-leave-them play-boy once. But for this moment he was all hers. She'd given up fighting the inevitable.

Ashraf stared down into eyes the colour of heaven and thanked all his lucky stars that he hadn't died that day fifteen months ago. One brief taste of this amazing woman was far too little.

Did she realise she'd called him Ash? As if time had peeled away and they'd just met?

In what he thought of as his exile years, deliber-ately courting scandal, he'd answered to Ash just to fit in more easily with the westerners with whom he partied. He'd automatically used the short form of his name when he met Tori.

But the way she said it, her voice soft with longing, was unique.

No other woman had made his name sound like that.

No other woman had made him feel this way.

He hauled Tori closer, losing himself in her bright smile and inviting eyes. In her scent, alluring and fresh as spring itself. In the sense of utter freedom, of tri-umph, that was his body's response to her invitation.

His clothes clung to her wet body, but the dampness couldn't douse the heat burning inside. He felt as if he'd waited for this moment half a lifetime.

Dragging his gaze away, he strode into the sitting room. Pillar candles had been lit in ornate lanterns and more candles were clustered on the table, where a feast was spread. The room looked romantic. Had Bram no-ticed Ashraf's frustration and decided to play Cupid?

Ashraf gave the room one brief, curious glance but kept going. In the bedroom, he was about to kick the door shut when he remembered Oliver. They needed to be able to hear if he cried out.

At the bed he slowly put her down, gratified when her hands stayed locked around his neck. She swayed, and satisfaction stirred at her neediness. It matched his.

Lamps cast the room in a golden glow, yet Tori outshone it. She looked vibrant, delectable.

Ashraf's hands slid up from rounded hips, past the inward sweep of her waist and around to her back. One tug and the back of the bikini top loosened. Her breath hissed but she didn't move, just stood, her fingers clasped at his neck. Her expression notched his ardour even higher.

It was a moment's work to undo the bikini top and drag it away. Now Tori's hands at his neck shook and her breasts wobbled. He felt unsteady himself, his lungs cramping at the sight of the bounty of her pearly flesh. Some small part of him was surprised that he, once reviled by his father as a voluptuary, was undone by the sight of a woman's breasts.

Reverently, greedily, he cupped them, their plump softness perfect in his hands. The rose-pink nipples were hard and trembling under the swipe of his thumbs. Tori bit her lip and he was torn between the need to capture her mouth again, to plunder her breasts or strip off the rest of her bikini and thrust himself deep inside her.

Ashraf bent to skim kisses around one breast. Tori's weight on his shoulders grew as she sagged closer. With one arm he caught her around the waist, pulling her to him. Her breathing roughened, hoarse and aroused, as he closed his lips around her nipple and sucked.

'Ash!'

It was a protest and a plea, possibly even a prayer.

And it shot all the blood in his body to his groin. He was buried in her scent, her flesh, her yearning. Needy fingers clamped his skull, pressing him closer as if she feared he might stop.

He did stop, but only to lavish attention on her other breast, drawing a groan from her that tightened his belly. Ashraf's need grew urgent, especially when Tori spread her legs around his and pressed close.

It was an invitation he couldn't resist.

Ashraf pulled back, ignoring her protest, and dropped to his knees. He smelled damp flesh, sweet woman and the musky, smoky scent of arousal.

His gaze fastened on her belly, which had once cradled his son. Pride, wonder and possessiveness gave added depth to carnal arousal. He stroked the tiny striations running across her skin.

'Stretch marks…' Her voice was breathless.

Wondering, he shook his head. 'You're amazing.'

Tori's laugh was uneven, as if she didn't believe him, but he was lost in wonder at the miracle her body had made and in sheer, blistering lust. He was afraid that if he wasn't careful he'd push her onto the floor and take her with the finesse of a rutting stallion.

Ashraf forced himself to slow, watching the contrast of his dark olive-skinned hand on her pale, satiny skin. But despite his best intentions his patience was negligible. Seconds later his fingers had insinuated beneath the narrow sides of her bikini bottom, sliding it down.

She was blonde there too, the damp V between her legs pale gold.

'I've found treasure,' he murmured, running his hands down her thighs and then back up and around to anchor in her buttocks. Her muscles squeezed beneath his touch.

Tori's hands were in his hair. He grabbed one, nipped the fleshy part of her palm with his teeth, then kissed the spot, feeling a voluptuous shiver race through her. She was deliciously responsive. So responsive that he couldn't resist leaning in and nuzzling the pale golden hair that pointed the way to Paradise.

'Ash!' Her voice was reedy and weak, but her grip spoke of robust feminine need as she tilted her pelvis forward.

Ashraf explored with his tongue in thorough strokes that turned her shivers to deep shudders. Her gasps were the most satisfying music and the perfume of her arousal was heady, beckoning him to delight.

He'd intended to take his time, to seduce her so thoroughly that he'd overcome her scruples about marriage. But now he discovered a flaw in his plans. He wanted her too much to wait. This time, at least. He had never felt so strung out. It shouldn't be possible, but he felt as if he'd spill himself here and now, bringing her to climax.

After a lingering kiss he pulled back and rose to his feet. Unfocussed eyes met his and satisfaction warmed him. He liked her dazed with need for him.

'Undress me, Victoria,' he ordered, enjoying the sound of her full name, an intimacy they alone shared.

His satisfaction cracked as she reached for his long robe and pulled it up his legs with clumsy hands. He liked her touch, but even the brush of her fingers tested his control, teasing him when he was already stretched to breaking point.

He'd left his shoes at the door, so when she lifted

his robe off he was bare but for silk boxers. This time Ashraf was the one to shudder as her gaze raked him. He felt it as if she'd stroked her slim fingers across his skin. He stood proud, lifting towards her, hardening still further.

'Your scar healed well,' she said finally.

Her touch slid along his ribs, tracing the knife mark. Where she touched he burned, as if she trailed ice over searing flesh.

'You haven't finished,' he gritted out, capturing her fingers and securing them in the waistband of his boxers.

Amusement flickered in her eyes. 'How remiss of me.'

But instead of pulling the offending garment away she sank to her heels before him. Ashraf's lungs atrophied at the sight of her there, naked and alluring, a carnal fantasy made flesh. His brain and lungs stopped when she tugged his underwear down and leaned in, taking him in her mouth.

Ten thousand volts jolted through him. He felt soft lips, moist heat, the tease of silken hair and then incredible, sweet delight as she drew hard on his flesh.

For a moment that lasted half a lifetime he gave himself up to carnal gratification. The feel of what she did to him, the sight of her there on her knees…it was too much.

Ashraf grabbed her shoulders and gently pushed her away, almost relenting when he saw her heavy-lidded eyes and moist lips.

'Later…' His voice cracked right down the middle.

'You didn't like—?'

'Of course I liked.' He sounded angry—probably

from the effort it took not to pull her back. 'But I want to be inside you. *Now.*'

A flush crested her cheekbones. Amazing, given what she'd just been doing. And charming. Utterly charming.

'Come.' Ashraf drew her to her feet.

They stood so close she swayed and he pulled her in against him, revelling in the slide of her body against his. Every part of his flesh was an erogenous zone. One more touch, one more look from this woman, might send him over the edge.

How exactly they got onto the bed he wasn't sure. And that was remarkable to a man used to taking the lead in sexual encounters.

Their legs entwined as they lay facing each other. The way she looked at him made his chest swell. But there was no time to ponder unaccustomed feelings. His need was too strong. Especially with delicate feminine fingers urging him nearer.

It was the work of a moment to roll her onto her back and settle between her splayed thighs. Ashraf's mouth curved in a tense smile. He appreciated her complete lack of coyness now she'd decided to stop fighting.

The only fight now was his own as he battled sensory overload—her silky skin, the beckoning heat teasing his groin, her piquant feminine perfume and the sight of her achingly beautiful breasts jiggling with each breath.

Tori stroked his shoulders restlessly, her eyes brilliant as gems. Ashraf knew he should take his time, savour every second, but he also knew his limits.

'Next time, *habibti*,' he murmured as he captured one of her hands.

'Next time what?'

'Next time we'll take it slow.'

He caught her other wrist and lifted both hands above her head, holding them with firm fingers. He watched her eyebrows lift, but though she could have broken his grasp she didn't try.

'I don't want slow.'

Her words ignited the blaze he'd tried to bank down. She'd barely stopped speaking when he pushed her thighs wider, grinding himself against her core. His gaze fixed on her face and the arrested expression there. Her look, the feel of their bodies together, were delight and torture together. More than flesh and blood could withstand.

'Nor do I.'

He slid his free hand between them, feeling her lush wetness, the hungry pulse of her body as he probed, hearing her swift intake of breath. A second later his hand was beneath her bottom, tilting her towards him as he bore down in one long, steady push that left him centred within her.

Sweat broke out at his nape and his brow. Muscles seized as the full reality of their joining penetrated his brain.

He had waited so long for her. Since that night in the desert he'd taken no lover, telling himself he was too busy. Now he understood with a flash of terrible insight that he hadn't wanted any woman but this one.

The realisation took a millisecond—less time than it took to draw breath. Yet it rocketed through him like the rush of a desert sandstorm, blanketing all thought.

Then primitive instinct took over.

Ashraf's mouth went to her breast, drawing hard, making her cry out and wrap her legs around his waist, rising against him in hungry desperation. A desperation that matched his own.

He erupted in a storm of movement. He withdrew and thrust harder, deeper than before, setting up a rhythm that matched the hammer beat of blood in his ears and the rough syncopation of their breathing.

It seemed only seconds before he felt the first fluttery tremors deep in her body. Setting his jaw and stiffening his arms, he tried to withstand the drag of delicious sensation as her climax shuddered through her. But the expression in those eyes locked on his, the sound of her desperate gasps, even the way she clutched him, as if he were the only solid point in a swirling universe, amplified the ecstasy he felt as she convulsed into orgasm.

'Ash! Ash, please!'

It was too late. Her pleasure became his. The clench of her muscles blasted him off the edge and into an oblivion so deep he knew nothing but the pleasure-pain of rapture.

When his senses returned he was trembling all over like a newborn foal. His pounding heart filled his ears and his strength was gone, leaving him plastered across her pliant body.

'Victoria…' It was a silent gasp against the fragrant skin of her throat. There was nothing else except this woman and the aftershocks of explosive passion racking a body he was sure would never move again.

She filled his every sense. He nuzzled her throat, needing even now to be connected to her. And then the hands grabbing his shoulders slid down his back. Her arms wrapped tight around his middle as if she, too, needed to be as near as possible.

She planted a kiss on his shoulder and he felt her lips curve. 'Thank you, Ash.'

With a superhuman effort he lifted his head. Forget-me-not eyes met his. They were heavy-lidded and she wore a dreamy smile. This was how he wanted her—sexy, warm and biddable. And the way she used the shortened form of his name pointed to another barrier smashing down between them.

Ashraf's mouth tilted up in an answering smile. 'Thank *you*, *habibti*.'

They might be together because of the child she'd borne, but he knew in the very marrow of his bones that this was the right thing.

His hold on her tightened.

His woman. Soon to be his wife.

CHAPTER TEN

TORI SIGHED AS pleasure trickled through her. The bed was soft, she'd had the best sleep she could remember and, half-awake, she sensed all was well with the world.

It took her a few moments to realise that the delightful sensation that had roused her was a trailing caress. The brush of fingers across naked skin.

Naked skin.

For a moment her dulled brain couldn't compute that till, in a flurry of excitement, memories swamped her.

Ashraf, even more potent and magnificent in the flesh than in her dreams, powering into her with a single-minded focus that had been almost as arousing as the feel of his hard body.

He'd been strong yet tender, urgent yet considerate. She trembled, recalling how his body had made hers sing. How his touch had reduced her defences to rubble. How the pleasure had gone on and on and—

'Ash!'

Her eyes popped open as that wandering hand strayed across her breast, pausing to circle in ever-diminishing rings towards her eager nipple.

Dark eyes held hers—eyes that danced with devilry and hunger. By the pearly light filling the room she knew it was very early morning and she felt a fillip of delight that Oliver had slept through, leaving her and Ashraf uninterrupted. Soon, she guessed, he'd wake…

Then Ashraf pinched her nipple and her thoughts shattered. Tori all but rose off the bed as arousal shot through her. His leg across hers held her down and even that, she discovered, excited her.

Mouth dry, she licked her lips. His eyes followed the movement. At his throat a tiny pulse flickered hard and the tendons at the base of his neck pulled taut.

Tori breathed in sharply, excited by his arousal. It was a heady thing, discovering she had power over this man she found impossible to resist.

'Good morning, Victoria.'

Even the way he said her name—her full name, that no one but her father used—tugged at unseen cords in her belly. She used the name Tori partly because its less feminine sound fitted her work environment, but mainly because she hated how her father expressed his disapproval by drawing out the syllables.

Now, on Ashraf's tongue, her name sounded sensual and inviting.

'Good morning, Ashraf.'

His hand slid down to circle her navel and feather her belly, drawing a shiver from her and an eager softening of muscles. Her legs quivered.

'Last night it was Ash.'

'Was it?' She remembered, but pretended not to. Because last night he'd flattened every barrier between them.

When they made love it was as if time ripped away and she was with Ash again, the vital, viscerally exciting man she'd known in the desert. The man who tried to protect her, who'd given her the gift of his support when she'd been terrified. Rather than Ashraf, the man whose intentions worried her, despite his attempts to allay her concerns. For nothing could take away the fact that he was supreme ruler in this foreign land and that he wanted her to relinquish her freedom and everything she knew.

If he knew the full extent of his power over her...

She shivered.

His hand paused just inches away from the apex of her thighs and, despite her worrying thoughts, Tori felt the sharp bite of frustration. No matter her concerns for the future, she needed more.

Tori pressed her palm down on the back of his hand, holding it against trembling skin.

Their eyes clashed.

'Why did you stop? You want me to call you Ash?'

Broad shoulders shrugged above her. 'Call me whatever you like.'

Yet he made no move to complete what he had been doing just moments before.

An ache set up inside her, deep in that hollow place he'd filled last night. And in her chest, as if her heart or lungs were bruised.

Tori shook her head, bemused by her imaginings. Yet she wasn't imagining the bone-deep yearning for completion. Or her lover's waiting stillness as he looked down at her.

Her lover. The words washed through her, and with them a kind of relief. Whether she thought of him as Ash the honourable stranger or Ashraf the determined King, she wanted him.

What more did he want from *her*?

She'd already proved she was no match for the desire he ignited in her. It was a mere week since he'd come back into her life and she was amazed she'd withstood his allure so long.

Desire made her limbs tremble as she looked up into eyes that beckoned and challenged at the same time.

Tori's mouth firmed. If he was waiting for her to say she'd changed her mind about marriage he'd have a long wait. Or was it something else he wanted?

She lifted her hand from his and cupped his shoulder, pushing him back. Her pulse accelerated with excitement as he let her, falling back onto the bed.

He lay there, big and bold and utterly still, like a bronzed cat lazily sunning itself in the pale light spilling across the rumpled bed. Yet there was nothing lazy in the eyes that meshed with hers. A frisson ran through her at the invitation she read there.

Shedding any hesitation, Tori rose to straddle powerful thighs. Ashraf was all heavy muscle and heat—incredible heat. His mouth tugged wide in a satisfied smile but otherwise he didn't move. Until Tori leaned forward to lick to one dark nipple and a tremor ran through his supine body. Hard hands grasped her hips. She licked again, then nipped with her teeth, hearing his breath catch as he lifted beneath her.

This time she took the lead. She brushed kisses across his torso, with its scattering of dark hair, then drew on his other nipple and heard what sounded like a low growl. His fingers tightened on her. Lifting her gaze, she found his eyes locked on her and a thrill of empowerment zigzagged through her.

Levering herself higher, Tori stretched up his body,

letting her breasts skim his chest. It felt so good she had to stop and stiffen her wobbly arms.

There was no laziness in Ashraf's face now. Watching the convulsive movement of his throat as he swallowed, feeling the swell of his arousal beneath her, Tori knew for the first time that he was at her mercy. It was delightful—if short-lived. For then Ashraf lifted his hips, letting her feel the full force of his appetite for her. Tori's pulse hammered in her throat, her lips firming over a moan of need.

'Ride me, *habibti*.'

So much for being the one setting the pace. But how could she object as he urged her up onto her knees? Besides, his voice was more gravel than velvet, and his hands on her hips betrayed his desperation.

Tori knelt above him, dragging out the moment of anticipation, one hand on that broad chest the colour of old gold. Beneath her palm his heart raced. That was what undid her—feeling Ashraf equally at the mercy of their mutual desire.

Closing her other hand around him, watching his hooded eyes, she lowered herself so slowly that the sensation of him rising to complete her seemed to take for ever.

When, finally, she rested fully against him, Tori experienced again that sense of quiet magic. As if time stood still in the presence of something extraordinary.

But it couldn't last. Already the need to move was unstoppable. Tori rose high, then slid down with an exquisite friction that made everything inside her quiver.

Ashraf's body was fiery hot, his eyes glittering fiercely as she moved again and again, arching in an instinctive dance against him. She set the pace and every movement took her closer to bliss.

The threads inside her body tightened, pulling into a coiling knot where every feeling converged. Then, without warning, a searing white light engulfed her. Tori heard a threadbare voice in the distance calling for Ash. Felt the sudden, cataclysmic wave of ecstasy and could do nothing but ride it out, her eyes locked on his.

She watched as the wave took him too. And the sight swept her from rapture to oblivion.

All Tori knew was the fire-burst of bliss and Ash—everywhere Ash, within her, around her, below her, his hands anchoring her, his body worshipping her, his rough voice praising her.

She didn't even remember falling. Just knew, as Ash's arms roped her to him and she inhaled the familiar cinnamon and spice scent of his skin beneath her cheek, that she never wanted to be anywhere else.

Ash emerged from the shower in Tori's suite wearing a mile-wide smile.

Life was good. The afterglow of spectacular sex filled him, but it was more than that. Everything was falling into place. He'd announce their impending marriage at the upcoming royal reception.

Now he'd cleared up Tori's fears that he'd hidden her and Oliver out of shame all would be well. He'd reassured her that she was free to make her choices and she'd chosen *him*, coming to him utterly of her own volition.

It was good that they'd had that confrontation. It had clarified things, allayed her doubts. And it had showed him another facet of his future wife. She was a woman who would stand for no insults against her son, a woman who'd defy anyone, even Ashraf, to protect Oliver. The way she'd argued her points, standing toe to toe with him, had aroused his admiration.

And his libido.

He grabbed a towel and rubbed his hair, remembering the spark in his belly as she'd faced him. Even his annoyance at her misconceived doubts hadn't quenched that.

Nor, he realised as he towelled his body, had a cold shower. Despite his heavy schedule he'd happily have spent another hour in bed with Tori. Only the sound of little Oliver, awake and hungry, had stopped him.

And even that interruption had its positives. Going to Oliver's room to find his son looking up at him curiously, Ashraf hadn't felt impatience but a surge of tenderness. Getting to know his child, having a real role in his life, meant everything to him.

Ashraf flung the towel away and dressed, his thoughts returning to Tori.

She was a strong mother. She'd make a superb queen, given time. And they had plenty of that—a lifetime.

Satisfaction warmed him—and the familiar pulse of desire. It was still early. There might be time before his first meeting...

No. He had other priorities. Namely, hearing Tori say she'd changed her mind about their future together.

Quickly combing his hair, he strode back to the bedroom—only to pause in the doorway.

Tori sat in bed while Oliver sucked at her alabaster breast. Lust pierced Ashraf. He recalled the taste of that breast, and the way his mouth on Tori's sensitive skin had catapulted her from languorous acquiescence to raw desperation. He breathed slowly, savouring the memory, and the peaceful picture of his woman and child.

Early sunlight turned her hair into a gilded angel's crown. Against the sumptuous coloured silks and satins her pale beauty shimmered like rare, fragile treasure. But her smile as she met his eyes sent a kick to his belly and told him that Tori was a robust, flesh-and-blood woman.

'I like watching the pair of you.'

The admission surprised him. He hadn't intended to say it aloud. At the sound of his voice Oliver half turned, then resumed feeding. A curious feeling filled Ashraf. Satisfaction? Excitement? And something bittersweet.

It seemed his son responded to him. That he recognised his father's voice.

Whose voice had Ashraf known as a child? Only his mother's, and then only for a short time. Oh, there'd been servants, even some kindly ones, but no adults to whom he was the wellspring of the world.

The only love he'd really known was his brother's. But Karim had been kept busy by their father, learning all that a future sheikh had to know. He'd had little time to spend with his kid brother, especially since he'd had to sneak time with Ashraf behind their disapproving father's back.

Ashraf would like Oliver to have a sibling. Several, if Tori agreed. He wanted Oliver to have the things he'd never enjoyed and would never take for granted.

'How do you feel about large families?'

Tori's brow furrowed, her smile fading. 'Why do you ask?'

Ashraf shrugged and walked to the side of the bed. 'We didn't used protection last night.'

At the time he'd been too busy exulting in how freely Tori gave herself to him. He hadn't paused for contraception. After all, they were to marry and he had no objection to more children.

'We didn't?' Her voice struck a discordant note and she suddenly sat straighter, making Oliver grumble. Her brow crinkled. 'No, we didn't, did we?'

Ashraf read her concern and understood. For Tori's sake a longer gap between children would be better. He'd seen her weariness and understood how pregnancy and single motherhood had taken a toll. There was no rush for more children. They had plenty of time.

'But they say the chances of getting pregnant are less while you're breastfeeding.' It sounded as if she was trying to reassure herself.

Ashraf reached down and touched her leg, stroking satiny skin. 'You're probably right.' Though he knew nothing of such things. 'And even if there is another baby sooner than we expected we'll manage together.'

'Sorry...?' Her eyes shone large and lustrous. But her expression wasn't what he expected.

'Next time you're pregnant...' He paused. 'Whenever that is, you won't have to manage alone. I'll be here to support you.'

Ashraf smiled and was surprised when she didn't reciprocate. Instead her features froze. Abruptly she closed her robe around her and put Oliver against her shoulder. Then she shuffled higher up the bed, sliding her leg away from his hand.

'There won't be a next time.'

'Sorry?'

'There won't be another pregnancy.' Tori paused, her breasts rising on a sharp breath. 'At least...' She shook her head. 'If it ever happens it will be far in the future. If I marry.'

'*If* you marry?' Ashraf saw her tilt her chin high and realised he was on his feet, looking down at her.

She shrugged, but there was nothing easy about the movement. She looked as rigid as he felt.

'Who knows what the future holds? If, later on, I fall in love, I might consider having another child.' She paused and glanced down at Oliver, nestled quietly at her shoulder. 'A brother or sister for Oliver *would* be nice one day...' she mused, as if the idea had just struck her.

Ashraf stared, outraged that she was still apparently rejecting him, even after tacitly accepting him last night. Forget tacitly. She'd been *blatant* in accepting him. Choosing him. Could she have been any more forthright? And that sultry smile she'd given him this morning as she straddled him...

His hands fisted as all his fighting instincts roused.

The idea of Tori, *his woman*, in love with some other man, *giving* herself to that unworthy stranger, filled him with a taste for blood he hadn't felt since he'd been a teenager, facing his father's sneering contempt.

'You gave yourself to me.'

His voice sounded strange, as if it came from a distance. Ashraf felt a constriction in his throat that matched the sudden cramp in his gut.

Her gaze turned to him and he watched understanding dawn.

'That was sex.'

She had the gall to make it sound like nothing.

'You wanted me. You accepted me.'

'Yes, I *wanted* you.' She said it slowly, enunciating each syllable. 'And you wanted me.' That was pure challenge—as was the flash of defiance in her fine eyes. 'But it was sex. It had nothing to do with...' Tori waved her hand, as if struggling to find the words.

Ashraf found them easily enough. 'My marriage proposal?'

Tori shook her head, her pale hair slipping around the deep rose-coloured robe that reflected the colour cresting her cheekbones. She wriggled to the side of the bed, holding Oliver close.

Ashraf caught tantalising glimpses of her slender thighs, then she stood, clutching her robe closed with one hand, the other cuddling Oliver.

'You never *proposed* marriage. You put it forward as a solution to a problem. Oliver isn't a problem.' Her voice rose to a wobbly high note.

Ashraf felt his forehead knot. What had happened to last night's passionate, accommodating woman? The woman who, he was sure, had finally agreed to be his?

Impossible as it seemed, his intended bride was rejecting him. *Again*. He clenched his teeth so hard that pain radiated from his jaw.

Never had a woman rejected him. Yet this woman made a habit of it.

'Is that what you want? Me on bended knee? Or would you prefer a candlelit meal with violins playing and a shower of rose petals? Would that satisfy you?'

Anger tightened every muscle. Disappointment, sharp as acid, blistered and scorched its way through his body.

And there was more.

Hurt.

Ashraf told himself it could only be hurt pride. He'd never considered offering any other woman what he offered Tori. His name, his honour, his loyalty.

'There's no need for sarcasm, Ashraf. I thought men were supposed to be good at separating sex and love or marriage.'

Despite the jibe, and the arrogant angle of her jaw, Tori's voice was brittle, her mouth a crumpled line. And abruptly, despite his roiling emotions, Ashraf realised something his anger had blinded him to.

Tori was scared. He read it in the obstinate thrust of her jaw and those over-wide eyes. In the protective way she held their son and the tremor she couldn't hide.

Scared of committing herself?

Or scared that he'd take Oliver?

That, as absolute ruler, he'd force her into a life that terrified her?

Drawing in air through his nostrils, Ashraf reminded himself that Tori barely knew his homeland except as a place of peril. He hadn't really helped her acclimatise. He'd deliberately left her alone during the day, believing she needed rest. And their evenings together had tested his determination not to seduce her.

How right he'd been. Sex had resolved nothing.

Tori hadn't tried to tease him or mislead him, giving him a night of unfettered passion and then withdrawing. She'd simply surrendered to a force too strong to withstand.

'Say something.' Her voice sounded stretched as if from tight vocal cords. 'What are you going to do?'

That was easy. He'd do whatever was necessary to secure Oliver and Tori.

Marshalling control, he smiled and watched her gaze drift to his mouth. 'I'm going to spend the day with you.'

And the next and the next. However many it took to convince Tori that life in Za'daq, with him, was the right choice. He'd court her till she stopped putting up barriers and surrendered.

CHAPTER ELEVEN

TORI LOOKED AT the vast landscape spread below the chopper and felt a mix of awe, curiosity and unease. The desert plain seemed to wash up to the edge of ragged mountains that fringed the border.

She gulped, tasting remembered fear. It was somewhere there that she and Ashraf had been abducted.

A warm hand closed around hers, making her turn to the man beside her.

'Okay?' The expression in those ebony eyes told her he understood the fear closing her throat.

Tori nodded, refusing to succumb to panic.

'I enjoy travelling by helicopter,' Ashraf added, as if suspecting she needed distraction, 'but I know some find it challenging.'

'I like it,' she finally admitted. She'd often flown to remote locations for work.

Why they were venturing so far from the city, she didn't know. Yet the opportunity to spend time with Ashraf, seeing him in his own environment, had been too precious to pass up. Tori had important decisions to make about Oliver's future. Getting to know Ashraf and his country was part of that.

Even if, after last night, part of her wanted simply to succumb to his demand for marriage.

If she'd known how profoundly making love to him would affect her she'd never have gone to bed with him.

Who did she think she was kidding? It would have taken a far stronger woman than she to say no. From the start he'd been irresistible.

She shivered and Ashraf stroked his thumb across her hand. Darts of arousal pierced low in her body. It worried her, how easily and how deeply she responded to him.

'Here we are.' He leaned across and pointed to a valley between two trailing spurs, where she saw traces of green and the sinuous curve of a river. 'That's our destination.'

'It's a long way to travel for a picnic.' When he'd suggested leaving Oliver behind for a couple of hours, she'd imagined they'd go to a beauty spot near the city.

His hand squeezed hers. 'I wanted you to see something of Za'daq apart from the capital.'

She turned to meet his eyes, trying to decipher that intent stare. 'And you wanted to show me how safe this part of the country is now?'

It was a guess, but the curling groove at one side of his mouth gave Tori her answer. He *had* chosen this location deliberately. Did he know she was still anxious about returning to the desert? Did he read her so easily?

'I don't want you afraid of shadows, Tori.' His eyes held hers. 'Plus, I want you to meet my people. For a long time this region hasn't had the benefits found in the rest of my country.'

The helicopter descended and he gestured towards

what looked like irrigation channels following the contours of the land, and a surprising amount of green vegetation.

'They are proud and hard-working. And things are changing here now Qadri has gone.'

Tori took a slow breath and nodded. She hated the anxiety niggling at her insides. Surely facing her fear would help her overcome that? It would be good to replace those terrifying memories with something else.

'I'll be interested to see them.'

Ashraf's smile as he threaded his fingers through hers made something hard inside her shift. Logic told her to keep some distance between them. He'd so readily assumed she'd changed her mind about marriage because she'd gone to bed with him. But she didn't have the energy to hold herself aloof. Basking in the warmth of his smile, in his company, was too tempting.

It was impossible to switch off the current of connection between them. Just this morning she'd gloried in his body and he in hers. She'd found heady delight and a sense of personal power in their lovemaking. How long since she'd felt powerful, much less mistress of her own destiny?

Since the kidnap she'd felt as if she was at the mercy of forces beyond her control. First her abductors, and then as her body altered to accommodate a new life, and later as she changed her life to put Oliver's needs first. She'd taken her current job so she could work child-friendly hours, not because she especially wanted to work there.

'Tori? Are you all right?'

Ashraf squeezed her hand. She looked around to discover they'd landed.

He leaned close, looking concerned. 'If you'd really rather go back…?'

But a crowd had gathered. A cluster of serious-faced older men in traditional robes, and behind them people of all ages.

'No. They're expecting you.'

From what she could see of the village, with its tumble of mud brick houses, Tori guessed a visit from their Sheikh would be a special event. She couldn't make him leave and disappoint them.

'How will you introduce me? Won't people wonder who I am?'

Ashraf grinned. 'Don't worry about that. Just come and meet them. Be yourself.'

Undoing his seatbelt and headset, he alighted from the chopper.

Tori hesitated, a hand going to her hair when she noticed most of the women wore headscarves.

'I'm not really dressed for this.' She'd worn a bright red top which usually made her feel good, but now it made her wonder if she should have dressed in a more conservative colour.

'You're perfect.'

His gaze lingered for a second, as if he could see through her loose-fitting top and summer-weight trousers. Instantly Tori's self-consciousness was swamped by awareness. Wind rushed in her ears and her breath snagged at the look in those gleaming eyes.

'Come.'

He reached out, took her hand and helped her down. The dying rotation of the helicopter's blades made her hair whirl around her face, but Ashraf didn't seem concerned that she looked slightly dishevelled. Presumably it didn't matter.

Then Tori had no time for self-consciousness as she was introduced not only to the village elders but it seemed to every adult in the place. Children stared up at her with wide eyes, but she was used to that. When she'd worked across the border in Assara, people had been fascinated by her pale colouring.

While Ashraf was deep in discussion with the elders one little girl, held in her mother's arms, swayed towards Tori, reaching out to her. Rather than pulling back, she let the child tentatively touch her hair.

The mother looked horrified, trying to draw away, apologising. But Tori shrugged and smiled. 'She's just curious. That's a good thing.'

The local schoolteacher, acting as interpreter, translated, and suddenly, instead of hanging back, more women approached. There was no more touching, but there were smiles and shy questions which gradually became a steady flow. Not, Tori was relieved to hear, about her relationship with the Sheikh, but about her homeland, so far away, and what she thought of Za'daq.

'If you'd care to take a seat, my lady?'

The teacher gestured as the small crowd parted and Tori saw, in the scanty shade of what appeared to be the village's only tree, a striped awning. Spread in the shade beneath it were richly coloured rugs and exquisitely embroidered cushions.

When they were seated a woman arrived with a bowl and a small towel. Another carried a jug of water, offering it to the guests to wash their hands. Then platters of food arrived—dried fruit and nuts, and pastries dripping with syrup. Coffee was prepared with great ceremony and offered in tiny cups.

'Thank you,' Tori said in their language. 'It's delicious.' She stumbled a little over the pronunciation but knew by the smiles around her that she was understood.

Ashraf turned and his expression warmed her even more than the pungent coffee.

'After this I'll inspect the irrigation scheme behind the village but I won't be too long. I promise to get you back to the city in good time.'

Because Oliver would be ready for a feed. It seemed incredible that a king would so readily fit his arrangements around that. As incredible as him changing his schedule at short notice to take her out.

'Would you like to come with me? Or you could stay here and chat? Or maybe see the school?' Tori saw him glance towards the teacher.

'I'll stay.' She turned to the teacher. 'Perhaps you could show me around?'

Her choice was a popular one. While most of the men went with Ashraf, the women and children accompanied her. The children pointed out places of interest like the well, now with a pump powered by a solar generator. And then there was the tower on the hill, which had brought modern communication to the valley for the first time. They also stopped to look inside one of the houses, where a loom was set up for silk weaving, and Tori admired the fine fabric.

The school was a one-roomed stone building. But to Tori's surprise it wasn't the bare little space she'd expected. It was well-stocked with books, colourful posters and a couple of computers.

Seeing her surprise, the teacher explained. 'The government is keen to ensure all Za'daqis have a good education. In remote areas where children can't travel to bigger schools we now have smaller schools, each supporting a village or two. In the old days children here didn't get any formal education.'

'It seems to be working well,' Tori said, watching the children talk to their mothers about the art on one wall. 'They seem very engaged.'

'They are. The difference here in just a couple of years is amazing.'

'Only a couple of years?'

'The school is very new.' He paused, as if choosing his words. 'Until Sheikh Ashraf there was no funding for local schools here. Now even the children in small settlements have access to education. It will give them a brighter future.'

Tori felt pride stir at his words, as if she had a vested interest in Ashraf's achievements. Perhaps she did. She was well past the stage of pretending indifference.

'Sheikh Ashraf tells me there have been a number of changes in the region?'

'There have, indeed.' The teacher said something to the women surrounding them and received nods and eager comments in response. 'Life is better here now, with plenty of food and even visiting doctors. It's peaceful too.' He shot her a sideways look. 'In the past there was a problem with evil men...lawless men who did bad things.'

Despite the warmth of the day ice slid down Tori's spine. 'Yes. I've heard about that.'

The man nodded. 'But now they are gone and we have the Sheikh's law. Things are much better. The people are safe.'

His words stayed with Tori through the rest of their visit, as she watched the boisterous children and the women's smiles. *Safe.* Ashraf made her feel safe too. Except for her doubts about accepting a convenient marriage and living in a country where his word was law.

When she was with him she felt different. Better. *Happier.*

Were those feelings enough to compensate for accepting a loveless marriage? She was surprised even to be considering it.

'Is everything okay?' Ashraf asked as the helicopter took off and they left the waving villagers behind. 'You're very quiet.'

It was because she was distracted by conflicting feelings. The more she learned of Ashraf, the more she understood his idea of marriage was rooted in good intentions. He didn't plan to take advantage of her.

Yet good intentions weren't always enough.

Tori looked down at the silk scarf on her lap, a kaleidoscope of sumptuous colour.

'This present is so beautiful but I didn't have anything to give in return.' It had been pressed into her hands by the woman whose house she'd visited—the silk weaver. 'Weaving is her livelihood and I'm not sure she can afford to give it away.'

Ashraf shook his head. 'Your interest in her life is enough. That is something these people haven't had much of in the past. Besides, they're proud. They brought out their very finest for our visit, but they didn't expect an exchange of gifts. You did the right thing, accepting this.' He paused. 'Don't worry. No one will be worse off because of our visit.'

Tori knew without asking more that he'd be as good

as his word. She leaned back in her seat and turned to watch the foothills slide into the distance. This time she felt no nervous tingle of apprehension at the sight.

'It sounds like they're already better off because of you.'

In her peripheral vision she caught his shrug. 'We've had some useful initiatives. They're beginning to bear fruit.'

'Like medical services, education, electricity and reliable clean water.' She ticked them off on her hand. Most men she knew would crow about their personal role in such successes. Her father especially.

Ashraf wasn't like the men she knew.

He caught her gaze and a surge of emotion enveloped her. Tenderness, yearning and something more. All sorts of feelings that she knew made her weak but which she couldn't suppress.

Ashraf captured her hand, setting off whorls of eager sensation just under her skin.

'What are you thinking, *habibti*?'

His voice had dropped to an impossibly deep note on the endearment.

Tori opened her mouth, about to give voice to the tremulous emotions that filled her. But at the last moment caution surfaced. She forced a casual smile. 'Just wondering how Oliver is doing with the nanny.'

Was that disappointment in his eyes?

The impression was gone in an instant, yet Tori couldn't banish the feeling that she'd been cowardly and less than generous with Ashraf.

That suspicion grew as her first week in Za'daq became a second. Instead of seeing Ashraf only in the evening she began to be taken out daily, introduced to his country and his people.

Despite her reservations, Tori looked forward to their outings and his company. She told herself she was relieved that he no longer pressed her to marry. Yet, to her chagrin, nor did he come to her bed.

Torn between pride and fear at how easily he dismantled her defences, she didn't dare initiate sex, not trusting herself. And that left her frustrated with herself and him. If it hadn't been for the smoking hot looks Ashraf sent her when he thought she wasn't watching, and his palpable tension when she stood close, Tori might have imagined him indifferent.

Was he trying to prove they could build a relationship based on more than sex?

She could only admire Ashraf's self-control. Hers frayed dangerously. Each day she fell further under the spell of this place and this man. And while Oliver settled into life in the palace she discovered so much in Za'daq to like.

Ashraf took her to the old parts of the city, with quaint buildings, narrow streets and hidden courtyards. They went to a vast covered market that sold everything from carpets and brassware to jewellery, perfumes and spices in all the colours of a desert sunset. Then to a dazzling art gallery, and a technology park where they visited fascinating new enterprises, and public gardens filled with families enjoying the green space. They drove out to a spectacular gorge where a rare breed of eagles nested and the scenery stole her breath as they watched the sun sink.

Tori met nomads in a desert encampment, traders, teachers and so many others who made her feel welcome. Wherever they went people were respectful but friendly, and gradually her nervousness about being in Ashraf's country eased.

He took her to a horse-trading bazaar on the edge of the city. Breeders had come from throughout the country and beyond, and the event had a holiday atmosphere. There was a great open-air feast and dashing displays of horsemanship. Tori watched in surprise when Ashraf agreed to take part, unable to take her eyes off him. He had the grace of a natural athlete, and when he rode it was like watching a centaur, man and horse moving as one.

It was late as they returned to the palace. The limousine's privacy screen was up, separating them from the driver, and Tori wished Ashraf would reach for her. She missed his touch. Missed the intimacy they'd shared. Her resolve to keep her distance was bleeding away like water in the desert sands and a new sort of tension filled her.

She turned to him, sucking in a sustaining breath as her pulse quickened. 'It was kind of you to give me such a lovely present but I really can't accept—'

'Of course you can. I watched your reaction when you saw that mare. It was love at first sight.'

Tori wrinkled her brow. If she didn't know better she'd say that Ashraf sounded *envious*. It was a bizarre thought that she hurriedly put aside.

'She's beautiful.'

It was true that Tori had fallen for an Arab mare being sold at the bazaar, but if she'd thought for a moment Ashraf would buy it for her she'd never have let her gaze linger on the gorgeous animal. She loved riding, but hadn't had a chance to indulge her passion for years, and it just wasn't practical now.

'But she needs someone who'll care for her full-time. I may not be here—'

Ashraf raised his hand and Tori was struck by the sudden austerity of his features. He looked handsome yet remote. More distant even than a week ago, when they'd argued after that glorious night together. When he'd believed she'd marry him because she'd gone to bed with him.

'She's yours, Tori. No strings attached. If you accept my offer and live here she'll be stabled at the palace. If you return to Australia she'll be shipped to you and I'll arrange stabling.'

It was the first time Ashraf had spoken of her possibly remaining in Australia. Instead of welcoming it as a sign that he'd finally seen reason Tori felt her stomach drop like a weight through a trapdoor.

She swallowed hard, trying to understand her reaction. Surely that wasn't disappointment she felt?

Increasingly she felt she clung to her determination not to marry out of obstinacy rather than anything else. But to marry without love—

The sound of her phone interrupted her agitated thoughts. Frowning, she fished it from her bag. She'd kept in contact with her friends via social media while in Za'daq. She wasn't expecting any calls.

'Victoria? Are you there?'

The familiar voice cut through her thoughts like shrapnel through flesh. He hadn't even waited for her to speak and that tone, the way he said her name, told her he wasn't happy.

Her lips flattened as she sat straighter. 'Hello, Dad. I'm afraid I can't talk. I'm—'

But it took more than that to stop Jack Nilsson. 'What are you playing at? Why did I find out from a bunch of diplomats that you're living with the King of Za'daq? I had to read it in the diplomatic post reports. The press there are already speculating about you and it won't be long before the media here gets hold of the story. *Then* what am I supposed to say?'

His voice grew more strident with every word and Tori shut her eyes, cringing at his tone despite the years she'd spent telling herself she wasn't responsible for his bad temper. She leaned back into the corner of the wide seat. She knew how her father's voice carried, especially when he was annoyed.

She shot a sideways glance to Ashraf and found him regarding her steadily. No polite fiction that he couldn't hear her every word. For a second she thought of simply hanging up—but her father would ring back, more incensed than ever.

'I told you Oliver and I were coming here.'

'But not to the bloody *palace*! You didn't even mention you knew the King, or that you were in a relationship. Are you *trying* to make me look like a laughing-stock?'

'Hardly.' The word was snapped out and actually succeeded in stopping the acid flow. 'I wasn't thinking about you when I agreed to come here.' She had been thinking of Oliver.

'You should have thought of me! You know there's an election looming. If I'd known you had such *personal* connections there, we could have pressed for exclusive rights in that Za'daqi mining exploration project...'

The rest of his words faded into a blur as nausea

rose. Her father had discovered she was the guest of a stranger on the far side of the world and his first thought was what he'd say to the press. His second was whether he could trade on her intimate relationship for commercial and thereby political gain.

Tori swallowed convulsively, fighting back bile. She should be used to her father's ways but sometimes he outdid himself in callous self-interest. There'd been not a word about how she was, or Oliver. How did he still have the power to hurt her even now?

'Dad, I can't talk privately.'

'Why? Aren't you alone? Is *he* there?'

Tori opened her mouth to say goodbye when a hand reached for the phone.

'If I may…?' Ashraf couched it as a question but there was no mistaking it for anything other than a command.

For a second she hovered on the brink of cutting the connection. Then she shrugged. Fine. The two alpha males could battle it out between them.

But as she listened to Ashraf's smooth voice she realised her father had met his match. Ashraf was gracious but firm, making it clear that their relationship was private, assuring her father that she and Oliver were safe and with every amenity at their disposal.

Her father's tone changed from blustering to friendly, almost eager. Tori rolled her eyes. He thought to use this situation for personal advantage. The idea made her queasy.

Ashraf ended the call and handed her the phone. 'He's concerned about you.'

'*Concerned* about me?' She shook her head, her

expression disbelieving. 'He's never been concerned about me—except to make sure I don't embarrass him publicly.'

Ashraf inclined his head. Tori's words confirmed his impression of the man.

'You don't like him?'

Nor did Ashraf. Her blustering father had turned slyly obsequious, talking about building stronger links between their countries. His concern for Tori and Oliver had been surface-deep.

'He's hard to like.'

'Go on.' He'd been curious about her relationship with her father, but hadn't pressed for details since he and Tori had other priorities. Maybe knowing more about it might help him understand her better.

'I'd rather not.'

Ashraf considered her steadily. 'I prefer to be prepared. He mentioned negotiating a marriage settlement.'

She goggled at him. 'He *didn't*? That's outrageous! I never mentioned marriage to him and nor did you.'

Ashraf shrugged. 'Nevertheless... I have a feeling he'll be calling my office again soon.' Not that he anticipated any difficulty in dealing with one whose motives were so transparent.

Tori sank back, rubbing her forehead, the picture of distress. 'I'm sorry.' She shook her head. 'I never—'

He reached out, capturing her hand, relishing its fit against his as he closed his fingers round hers. 'You've nothing to be sorry about, Tori.'

She met his eyes and sighed. She looked so upset Ashraf almost told her it didn't matter, that they didn't need to discuss this, but instinct told him it was important.

He waited patiently as the car drove towards the palace.

'He's completely self-focused,' she said at last. 'He married my mother for money and her family's political leverage. He wasn't interested in us, except to trot us out as the perfect family when it was time to impress the voters or the VIPs.'

Ashraf heard the hurt she tried to hide and vowed that Jack Nilsson would learn to respect his daughter.

'Fortunately my mother was lovely. We were close.'

Presumably it was from her mother that Tori got her sweet, honest character.

'Your father…he hurt you?'

'Not physically.' She paused. 'Really, I was lucky. He wasn't around much. He was away when parliament sat and the rest of the time he had other priorities.'

As if his family wasn't a priority. Ashraf's teeth clenched. He hated the idea of Tori with an uncaring parent. Yet surely that should make her more willing to create a real family for Oliver?

'Everything I did was judged on how it would look. I wanted to play soccer but he thought it more lady-like if I learned piano.' She shook her head. 'As a kid I couldn't get dirty or be seen in public with a hair out of place. It was extreme and unnecessary. I knew other politicians' kids who didn't live like that, but he saw me as an extension of himself. Everything was about appearance, not about being a real family. Our only value was as props to make him look good.'

Tori grimaced.

'I think eventually it destroyed my mother. She stayed with him because of me. She thought any family was better than none. But I *know* we'd have been better just the two of us, without him.'

Now Ashraf began to understand. Did Tori see parallels between his proposal that they marry to create a family for Oliver and her mother sticking at a bad marriage for her child's sake? Worse, did she compare his motivations with her father's?

The idea revolted him.

'And even now he tries to manage your life?'

Tori laughed, the sound sharp. 'Hardly! I rebelled when my mother died and I went to university. He wanted me to study law and follow in his footsteps.'

'But you chose geology.' He smiled. 'An act of rebellion *and* a chance to get your clothes dirty?'

Her chuckle warmed him, expelling the chill he'd felt since they'd begun this conversation.

'You could be right. It also gave me a career that would take me far away from him.'

'When you found yourself pregnant you didn't seek his assistance?'

He found it perplexing that she'd moved to the opposite side of Australia from her father. Without family support things must have been tough.

Her hand twitched in his, as if she'd withdraw it. Ashraf placed his other hand on hers, holding it steady. 'What is it?'

Her gaze met his then slid away. 'I told him what had happened and he told me to abort the baby. He said there was nothing to be gained from having it and that it would make it hard for me to secure the right sort of husband.'

Ashraf's hands tightened around hers. His throat choked closed on a curse. He drew a slow breath, searching for calm. 'Maybe he thought a permanent reminder of what you'd been through—'

'Don't try to excuse him!' Tori's voice rose to a keening note. 'He wasn't interested in me or how I was doing. He didn't even want me to see a counsellor in case my story leaked to the press.' She shook her head. 'He said my behaviour was *sordid*. He washed his hands of me and he has no interest in Oliver.'

Indignation exploded through Ashraf. Tori had been kidnapped and traumatised and the best her father had been able to do was tell her to abort the baby. He knew by her expression that her father had said far more too. Had he blamed Tori for what happened?

For her sake Ashraf had to stifle his incandescent fury. With difficulty he sat, outwardly calm. Yet he imagined getting his hands on the man who'd dared talk of marriage settlements and closer relations when he hadn't the common decency to care for his own flesh and blood.

'In that case you're better off without him. While you're in Za'daq I can make sure you never have to deal with him again.' It was little enough, but he'd take pleasure in doing it for her.

She nodded. 'Thank you.'

It was a good thing for Jack Nilsson that he was on the other side of the globe. Ashraf wasn't a violent man but he'd enjoy making an exception in this case.

No wonder Tori was wary of a pragmatic marriage. He'd mentioned the importance of public perception in Za'daq and maybe she assumed his motives were like her father's. The idea sickened him.

He stroked his fingers down her hot cheek, then lifted her chin so she had no choice but to meet his eyes.

'I give you my word, Tori. I'm not like your father.'

'I know that.'

But her smile was crooked. It cracked his heart to see her look that way. He was used to her being defiant, strong and independent. He hated it that perhaps some of the pain he read on her face was because of *him*.

'I make you a promise, Tori.' He placed one hand over his heart, his expression grave. 'If we marry I will be devoted to you and our children. Always. To be Sheikh is a privilege and an honour, but I know, I *understand* that family is more important than power and prestige.'

How could he not know? He'd grown up unloved and unregarded except by his brother. Ashraf would have given anything to have had an atom of love or even liking from his father. Or a genuine memory of a mother's tenderness.

'My family will be the centre of my life. You have my word on it.'

CHAPTER TWELVE

FOUR DAYS LATER Ashraf's words still echoed in Tori's ears. She recalled each nuance, the deep cadence of his voice, the searing look in those impossibly dark eyes, the feel of his hands, hard and warm but so gentle, clasping hers.

He'd made her feel cared for.

Special.

Tori bit her lip. She'd never been special to anyone except her mother. It was a strange feeling, both wonderful and nerve-racking.

If she believed him.

That wasn't fair. She *did* believe Ashraf. He meant every word. Tori had no doubt his intentions were good. But would good intentions be enough when his heart wasn't engaged? For, despite the shivery excitement his words, his look, his intensity had conjured in her, it was impossible to believe that after spending just a few short weeks together the King of Za'daq had fallen in love with her.

And without love how could she commit to marriage? She knew what a lack of love did to a family.

Yet Ashraf wasn't her father. He'd told her that but she'd known it from the first. Ashraf was—

'What's taking you so long, Tori? Do you need help with the zip?'

Azia's voice came from the bedroom, jerking Tori into the present. She blinked and took in the unfamiliar image in the mirror. It had been so long since she'd dressed up she barely recognised herself. And she'd never looked as she did in this dress.

'Just coming,' she called, smoothing her palms down the black velvet. It was reassuringly soft…like Ashraf's voice when they made love.

The thought sent another flurry of nerves jittering through her. Instead of making life easier, abstinence from sex had left her a wreck. The wanting hadn't stopped. It grew stronger daily. Especially since she knew Ashraf slept in the room neighbouring her own bedroom, connected to hers by a single closed door.

She caught her wide eyes in the mirror and dragged in air. This wouldn't do. She couldn't think about that if she was going to get through tonight's reception.

Smartly she stepped across the tiled floor and opened the door to the bedroom, sweeping in, her long skirts flaring. Azia waited, looking fabulous in the shimmery lime-green that complemented her sable hair and dark eyes.

'Ah…' Azia drew the syllable out, gesturing for Tori to turn. Obediently she did. When she faced her friend again, Azia nodded. 'Perfect. You'll stun them all.'

'That's what I'm afraid of.' Tori grimaced. 'You're sure it's not too much?'

'Too much?' Azia laughed. 'You're the guest of one of the richest men on the planet. How much is too much?'

'Well, the glitter, for a start. Though I love the silver embroidery. It's exquisite.'

Azia nodded. 'It's some of the best work I've seen, especially given how little time they had to make it.'

The dress had been made by a friend of Azia's, a designer just starting her own business with a couple of seamstresses.

'I wouldn't change a thing.'

'It's not too revealing?'

Tori had wondered about that, but left the detail to the designer, who'd been so excited and grateful to make a gown for a formal court event. Tori had told herself a local designer would know what was appropriate in Za'daq. But the narrow silver straps over her shoulders left a lot of bare flesh.

'Does it *feel* revealing?'

Tori shook her head. It felt wonderful. If she weren't so nervous she'd feel like Cinderella heading for the ball. She'd never possessed a dress so glamorous, or one that made her feel beautiful.

'Of course it doesn't.' Azia's tone was firm. 'The neckline's not too low and though the dress is contoured to your body it's not tight. You look sophisticated and elegant. I can't wait to see the look on Ashraf's face.'

The thought of him washed heat across Tori's cheeks but Azia, bless her, pretended not to notice.

'I'm glad you chose black instead of the deep red. It's perfect with your colouring. Besides,' she added with a twinkle, 'you can wear red for the next one. Or maybe that gorgeous kingfisher-blue we saw.'

Tori smiled automatically but her heart wasn't in it. Would there *be* a next time? She remembered Ashraf talking about having her horse shipped to Australia. And he hadn't pressed her again to accept marriage.

Maybe his offer for her to stay in Za'daq was no longer on the table, with or without marriage. She couldn't expect it to be open-ended. There must be limits to Ashraf's patience.

Yet returning to Australia didn't appeal. Was she getting used to a life of royal luxury? Of ease and comfort?

More likely she was growing used to basking in Ashraf's attention. The more time they spent together, the harder it was to imagine leaving. Even if it was for her own good. Ashraf was more, so much more even than she'd imagined.

A knock sounded on the door and before she could answer Azia was there, curtseying low.

'Your Majesty.'

Ashraf stood framed in the door, looking debonair and so handsome that Tori felt her insides roll over. She'd expected him to wear traditional robes tonight but instead he wore a dinner jacket, superbly cut to his rangy, powerful frame. The crisp white shirt accentuated the rich bronze of his throat and his hair shone black as jet.

'Majesty? Why so formal in private, Azia?' He took the other woman's hand and pulled her upright.

Azia dimpled up at him but her eyes were serious. 'Just practising my curtsey for tonight. I'm told I still haven't got it right.'

Ashraf frowned and kept hold of her hand. 'I can imagine who told you that. Just ignore them. I'd rather have your genuine smile than perfect court etiquette.' He paused. 'Just as I'd rather have your herbed lamb with lemons and pilaf than any ten-course royal feast.'

Azia blushed. 'Then you must come to dinner again soon. I'll talk to Bram about setting a date.' She darted a look at Tori. 'I'd better go. He'll wonder where I am. See you there, Tori.'

Then she was gone, surprising Tori, who'd expected to accompany her to the reception.

The door closed and Ashraf faced her. There it was again. The throb of sensation as if all the oxygen had rushed out of the room while heat pooled low in her body. She should be used to it. Instead of familiarity lessening the impact of Ashraf's presence, it only heightened her response.

'Victoria.'

His voice was a rough purr, drawing out the syllables of her name into something exotically beautiful.

'You look magnificent.'

She felt her shoulders push back, her lips curve at the extravagant compliment. 'Thank you. So do you. Though I expected to see you in traditional robes.'

He paced towards her. It felt as if the room shrank till there was nothing beyond Ashraf.

'It's good to mix things up. A change from tradition and court formality can be useful occasionally.'

Tori read the lines still bracketing his mouth. 'Is this something to do with Azia? With the people who don't think she and Bram are good enough to be here?' She'd finally prised that out of her friend and still reeled from what she'd learned.

'Some of the older courtiers look askance at anyone different, or any change. But they'll learn.'

The determined set to Ashraf's jaw told its own story. Tori knew Ashraf would make that change happen. Azia had explained how Ashraf and Bram had become friends—one a prince, the other literally a pauper.

Bram's mother had been a servant and his father a foreigner who'd left her pregnant, unmarried and struggling to feed herself, much less a baby. She'd been shunned and Bram's blue eyes had been a constant reminder of her shame. Doing his military service with Bram, Ashraf had saved him from a vicious whipping by some men who had objected to serving with a clever upstart from the gutter. Bram still bore scars from the attack, but he and Ashraf had been stalwart friends since.

The tale had left Tori seething with outrage. And warmed by Ashraf's actions and the men's friendship.

She blinked now as Ashraf moved into her personal space, pulling something from his pocket. A small leather box.

Tori's heart leapt. Surely he wasn't—?

'For you to wear tonight.'

Once more that low voice curled through her, like smoke caressing her senses. She breathed deep, registering Ashraf's warm cinnamon scent, and knew that soon she'd be begging for more from him. Days of companionship and those searing, unsettling looks had done nothing to satisfy her craving.

Slowly she opened the box and found a pair of stunning earrings. 'Are they...?' She peered more closely.

'Diamonds and obsidian.'

The diamonds were large and exquisitely cut, and beneath them the long teardrops of pure black obsidian were flawless.

'I've never seen anything like them.' She might be a geologist, but she usually saw stones in their raw state. She estimated that these were unique and incredibly expensive. Yet it wasn't their monetary value that mattered. It was Ashraf's expression as he offered them.

Her heart stilled. Could it be...?

'You like them?'

Ashraf cringed inwardly at the neediness of that question. Like a kid seeking validation from an adult, or a lovesick youngster mooning over a girl he could never have.

Yet he knew Tori would eventually come to him. He'd seen hints that she'd begun to see the sense of his arguments. Plus there were clear signs of her sexual frustration. Her hungry stare as he entered the room had been like an incendiary flare. He still felt the sparks in his blood.

'They're stunning. But I can't—'

'Of course you can. And it would please me if you wore them.' He paused, watching her waver. 'Azia will be disappointed if you don't. She made a point of telling Bram what colour you were wearing, knowing he'd tell me.'

Tori's mouth rucked up ruefully. She liked Azia, which pleased him. Azia and Bram had kept him sane these last couple of years since he'd taken the throne. True friendship was in scarce supply in the royal court.

'In that case, thank you.'

Colour streaked her cheekbones. Ashraf knew she wasn't used to accepting gifts. He liked that. Liked knowing she'd never been beholden to other men. She'd been shocked when he had procured that horse for her, protesting at length though it had been clear she adored the mare. His Tori was very independent but he enjoyed giving her presents.

He watched her replace her plain silver studs with the new earrings. As she turned the light caught the gems, drawing attention to the pale pearl lustre of her skin and her slender throat.

Ashraf's pulse quickened.

His. His magnificent Victoria.

She *would* be his—and soon.

Not just because she was the mother of his son. But because he wanted her. He'd never want any other woman but her.

It should have been a shocking revelation. Instead the knowledge was like the final piece of a puzzle slotting into place. Ashraf felt a buzz of excitement and at the same time the peace of acceptance.

His gaze fell past pale skin down to a dress that glittered like the fathomless night sky in the desert, awash with stars. Traceries of delicate silver thread gave way to pure black where the dress skimmed her gorgeous body.

Ashraf swallowed hard. His baser instincts urged him to forget the people already gathered in the royal audience chamber. He'd rather spend the evening here with Tori.

He read her eyes, which had turned misty with awareness. It would take little to persuade her into bed…

But he had a duty to his people. A duty to Tori. To show her what her world would be like in Za'daq. That included events like tonight—not as much fun as visiting a souk or a village. She had to know the worst as well as the best. He just hoped, with a nervousness he hadn't felt in years, that the reality of court life didn't terrify her.

As expected his arrival, with Tori on his arm, caused a ripple. Cronies of his father raised eyebrows and matrons who'd shoved their unmarried daughters in his direction since he'd ascended to the throne barely hid their chagrin.

Ashraf surveyed them undaunted from his superior height. Tori was his personal guest. When she married him people would have to accept his choice.

None of them were courageous enough to say what was on their minds. That the woman at his side wasn't a Za'daqi aristocrat. That he'd actually *touched* her in public—even if it was just a guiding hand on her elbow. That he'd broken custom by wearing western clothes.

They'd put up with his changes to government policy because even the most hidebound had begun to see the benefits. But alterations to court tradition, and by extension to their own sense of superiority, would be harshly judged by some. There had already been dismay because he'd been seen holding Tori's hand on a rural visit.

However, he sensed change wouldn't be as difficult as it had been when he'd inherited the throne. His nation was altering. Ashraf had enjoyed the evening more than usual. There was a wider mix of social groups and foreigners attending. Plus the atmosphere became more relaxed after the crowd had gone outside to watch feats of horsemanship, archery and acrobatics. He'd seen Tori's delight and viewed it all through new eyes, enjoying her enthusiasm.

Now, late in the reception, he was enjoying a joke with an army officer who'd been a friend in the old days. When he'd believed he'd found his future in the military. Before his father had cut short his career, outraged at the thought of the despised cuckoo in the nest excelling at something.

Ashraf saw Tori, stunning in silver and black, eyes bright as she laughed with Azia, another woman and a man he recognised as a foreign diplomat. Tori was gesturing towards Ashraf, as if pointing him out.

At that moment an older couple broke in on the group. The irascible Minister for the Interior and his haughty wife. They spoke and Azia flushed furiously. Tori's chin lifted. The two foreigners with them looked startled.

Ashraf started forward but a voice in his ear said, 'No. Wait.'

It was Bram.

'Is there a problem?' his army friend asked, craning to look past the crowd.

'Only a little one,' said Bram. 'Not worth worrying about. Besides, I think… Yes, it's taken care of now.'

He was right. Whatever poison the older couple had tried to spread clearly hadn't worked. Tori was speaking now and his nemesis looked discomfited, his wife embarrassed. Then Tori and the foreign woman began chatting again. Colour flushed Tori's cheeks but otherwise she looked serene.

'Nevertheless, I'll make sure,' Ashraf murmured. 'If you'll excuse me?'

He reached the group and all eyes turned to him. The Minister opened his mouth to speak but Tori was faster.

'Your Majesty.'

Tori said it as easily as if she called him by his title daily. Her eyes glittered bright as diamond chips, and the slight flare of her nostrils hinted at displeasure, but otherwise her expression was calm, her smile welcoming.

'I don't believe you've met Ms Alison Drake, the new American ambassador.' She turned to the slim brunette, 'Alison, I'm pleased to introduce you to His Majesty Sheikh Ashraf ibn Kahul al Rashid of Za'daq.'

Not by a flicker did Ashraf betray surprise at her remembering his full name, or at her deft handling of the introduction. Hadn't she spent her youth at her father's side, mingling at official functions?

'Ms Drake, it's a delight to meet you.' He shook her hand, preventing her from curtseying. 'I understood your flight had been delayed? I expected you tomorrow.'

'The pleasure is mine, Your Majesty. Apologies for my very late arrival. I managed to get an alternative flight and was advised...' she glanced at her companion from the embassy '...that it would be okay to attend—though I haven't yet formally presented my credentials.'

The Minister for the Interior cleared his throat but Ashraf silenced him with a look. He had no role in diplomatic matters and he'd tried to stir up trouble for Tori and Azia. Ashraf wouldn't tolerate that.

'Of course. It's a pleasure to welcome you. We'll leave the formalities till tomorrow. In the meantime, I hope you're enjoying yourself?'

'Oh, yes. I've had such a wonderfully warm welcome to your country.'

He didn't miss the way her eyes flickered towards the older man. Or how Azia bit her lip and focused on adjusting her shawl. His curiosity deepened.

'Excellent. Let me introduce you to some more people.' He looked across the crowd to Bram, who was already ushering forward a number of dignitaries to meet the ambassador.

Ashraf turned to the couple standing stiffly to one side. 'Minister, your wife looks very tired.' He offered her a charming smile and watched her swallow nervously. 'You have my permission to leave. We'll talk tomorrow.'

It was hours before Ashraf could be alone with Tori.

The guests had been encouraged to leave and the staff had shut the doors, leaving them the sole possessors of the audience chamber. They stood before the large arched windows looking over a city washed in the national colours of crimson and gold from a final flourish of fireworks.

But Ashraf's eyes were on Tori, not the view. She'd never looked more beautiful. Nor had the connection between them, invisible as spun glass but strong as the desert sun, been more palpable. She'd spent the last part of the evening at his side and it had felt right.

It was where she belonged.

Tonight, for the first time in a week, he dared to hope she felt the same. The way she smiled at him, the sense of understanding, the fizz in his blood when their eyes met, had to mean something.

Any fear he'd felt that she might be scared off by the pomp of a royal event had been short-lived. She'd shone. She was charming and interested in people. Those qualities had endeared her to his people on their excursions. Plus those years of supporting her father had stood her in good stead.

'You were magnificent tonight.'

He caught and held her hands. Their eyes met and he felt the impact square in the centre of his chest.

She shook her head, her mouth curving up. 'That was you, Your Majesty. Magnificent.'

He tugged her closer, almost close enough to kiss. But there was one matter to clear up first.

'What was that scene with the Minister for the Interior?'

Tori's eyebrows pinched. 'You saw that? I didn't think anyone had noticed.'

'That he'd been insulting?' Again, Ashraf felt fury burn. 'I don't think anyone else did—only me and Bram.'

Both had been watching their womenfolk. Yet only Bram had been sure that the women could handle the problem. Ashraf had underestimated Tori.

'You handled him well. Now, tell me.'

She sighed. 'He had no idea who Alison was. He saw us laughing and assumed she was simply a friend of mine or Azia's and therefore unimportant.'

Ashraf had learned tonight that the ambassador had once been posted to Australia. She was an old friend of Tori's mother.

Tori lifted her shoulders. 'He made disparaging remarks about court standards slipping since shopkeepers and…and others had been invited to such events. He suggested we leave as we must feel out of place.'

Ashraf understood the reference to shopkeepers. Azia's parents ran a shop in the main souk. But 'others'…

'Others?' He was sure the colour washing Tori's face had nothing to do with the fireworks. His jaw clenched. 'Tell me.'

'I've forgotten his exact words.'

Tori wasn't a good liar, but before he could call her on it she continued.

'He lost his air of superiority when I stared him down, mentioning how kind and welcoming most Za'daqis were to guests.'

Ashraf didn't miss the emphasis on *most*.

'I introduced him to the new ambassador and Alison mentioned that her parents had run a grocery store back in the States.'

Despite his anger, Ashraf laughed. Hospitality was something Za'daqis prided themselves on. The Minister would have hated being called out on his rudeness. 'I like your friend Alison more and more. Nevertheless, I want to know—'

Tori put her finger to his mouth, stopping his words. Touching him felt so good. How had she kept her distance this last week?

'I'd rather forget him. He's rude and self-opinionated— but you know that.' She felt Ashraf's surprisingly soft lips against her flesh and longing shivered through her. And something more profound. 'Don't let him spoil what's been a wonderful night.'

'Wonderful?'

Eyes gleaming, Ashraf captured her wrist and kissed her palm, turning that shiver into a pounding torrent of awareness.

Tori gulped, her throat closing as she looked into that strong, dear face.

She prided herself on her honesty and her willingness to face facts, no matter how unpalatable. But tonight she realised she'd hidden from the truth.

Far-fetched as it seemed, if she counted on the calendar the time they'd actually spent together, Tori was in love with Ashraf al Rashid.

In love. Not just in lust. Not just admiring of his determination to do right by Oliver and his people or grateful for his understanding of her doubts.

In love.

Totally.

When he'd given her these fabulous earrings and she'd caught his tender look the truth had struck. She'd wondered if his feelings were more deeply engaged than she'd suspected. Had she resisted his proposal so adamantly because she cared too much for him? Because she didn't want to commit herself till she knew he felt the same way?

The thought of loving Ashraf but never having his love terrified her. It was a roiling wave in her belly whenever she dwelled too long on doubt. But tonight, as she watched him with his people and basked in his attention, she couldn't hide from her feelings any longer.

If her abduction in the desert had taught her one thing it was to live for the moment. You never knew what was around the corner. Whether you'd have another chance to do what really mattered.

What really mattered was Oliver and Ashraf.

'Victoria? You're miles away.'

Ashraf curled an arm around her waist, securing her against him, and everything inside her rejoiced. *This* was where she wanted to be.

She licked her bottom lip and saw his eyes zero in on the movement. Heat drenched her. But as well as physical need she recognised now the deeper sense of contentment that swelled her heart.

Life in Za'daq would have challenges. Life with

Ashraf would be a learning experience. But love couldn't be denied. She'd made up her mind.

'I've come to a decision.'

Ashraf's grip tightened, his brows furrowing. 'Don't let one bigoted man—'

'Shh…' She reached up on tiptoe and silenced him, this time with her lips. How she'd longed for his kiss!

He gathered her in with both arms and would have deepened the kiss but Tori leaned back just enough to speak. She felt secure in his embrace—not because she needed protection or looking after but because Ashraf made her feel as no other man had. Because she loved him.

'If the offer is still open, I'll marry you.'

For a moment she thought he hadn't heard. Or that she hadn't said it aloud, just thought the words. He looked down at her, his expression unreadable.

Then, to her amazement, he dropped to his knee. Her hands were in his and he kissed first one and then the other. Not in passion but with a deliberate reverence and a formal courtesy that belonged in a world of warrior knights and beautiful maidens.

'You have my word, Victoria, that you won't regret this.' His voice made it a solemn vow. 'I will do all in my power to make you happy. To support you, honour you and care for you. And our family.'

His words sent a flurry of emotion through her.

Care. That was good. More than good when combined with the rest of his promise.

Tori shut down the querulous inner voice that said care wasn't love. That the chances of Ashraf ever loving her were slim, given how he'd grown up unloved. The fact that he loved Oliver was enough for now. It had to be. And maybe, just maybe, over time—

Her thoughts stopped as Ashraf surged to his feet. That sombre expression had vanished, replaced by a smile so brilliant it undid something inside her.

'Thank you, Tori.'

Then, before she realised what he was about, Ashraf swooped low, scooping her up in his arms, swirling her around and striding across the room.

She laughed. 'Where are we going?'

As if she didn't have a fair idea.

'To bed. To show you how good our marriage will be.'

Because he was afraid she'd change her mind? No. She'd decided. She wouldn't expect the impossible. Tori would accept what was offered and make the most of it.

She didn't believe in fairy tales.

CHAPTER THIRTEEN

ASHRAF SEETHED AS he marched into his office. There'd been satisfaction in sacking the Minister for the Interior, but not enough.

'Meeting didn't go well?' Bram looked up from his desk.

'It went as expected. We now have an opening in the Ministry.' And an offended ex-minister, shocked that his King had actually dismissed him. The old goat had thought himself untouchable.

'Good. The Council will run better without him.'

Ashraf shoved his hands in his pockets. 'I expected you to counsel patience.' That had run out last night.

Bram shrugged. 'You gave him chance after chance, compromising to bring the old guard along with you and allow him some pride. But he's dead wood, holding the government back.'

Ashraf lifted his eyebrows. Bram really was speaking his mind today. 'What's happened?' He knew his friend. Something had prompted his militant attitude.

Bram nodded to his computer. 'The press reports are worse than we first thought. Somehow they've got a photo of Tori and Oliver, taken in Australia. Speculation is rife that he's your son.'

Ashraf ploughed his fingers through his hair. It had been a gamble, waiting to legitimise Oliver. Ashraf had wanted to announce a wedding simultaneously, but he'd respected Tori's need for time.

'The cat's out of the bag, then.' He took a deep breath. 'Arrange a press release. I'll—'

'That's not all.' Bram looked grim. 'I've received a petition from a small group of Council members. They've heard about Oliver and know that you've moved out of your apartments to be with him and Tori. They insist you give them up or abdicate.'

Ashraf snorted. 'As if they have the power to *insist*! Let me guess.' He named three cronies of the sacked Minister and Bram nodded. 'They seem to forget it's only by *my* pleasure that they have a role in government.'

'They threatened to approach Karim and ask him to assume the throne.'

Ashraf gritted his teeth. The last thing Karim wanted or needed was a delegation of old fogeys bothering him. 'Karim rejected the throne. He can't simply change his mind. Even if it were possible, he'd never agree.'

Bram lifted one eyebrow but Ashraf said no more. Only he and his brother knew the reason for his action. A medical test had revealed that Karim, not Ashraf, was the cuckoo in the nest, the son of another man.

Privately Ashraf thought that had precipitated his ailing father's death. The revelation that the son he'd groomed as heir wasn't his while the despised younger child was his true son.

Karim had stayed after the funeral only long enough to see Ashraf crowned and then left Za'daq. He had no plans to return.

'Is that all?'

'One of the latest press reports has a particularly nasty edge. It makes a great deal of Tori's work in isolated areas, often as the only female on a team. It draws conclusions about her morals and insinuates...'

Bile rose in Ashraf's throat. 'I can imagine. Where, precisely, was this from?'

Bram mentioned a media outlet owned by a friend of the sacked Minister. Ashraf nodded. 'Show me, and call the legal office. They can check the libel laws.'

He'd end this *now*, before it came to Tori's ears.

But as the afternoon wore on Ashraf's fiery indignation was overtaken by something far harder to bear. Especially when the lawyers dithered over whether the law had actually been broken. Ironically, if Tori were Za'daqi, or if she'd already married him, the reports could have been taken down and the outlet closed. As a foreigner, her situation was less clear.

Ashraf had grown up being vilified by his father. He was used to people assuming the worst about him. But to see Tori belittled and be unable to stop it tore at something vital within him.

He stalked the offices, trying to find a solution but finding none. He either abided by the laws he'd introduced, allowing more freedom for the press, or he gave up all pretension of being anything other than an autocratic ruler, thus destroying the hard work he'd put into turning Za'daq into a more democratic country.

He was caught by his own insistence on reform, and his inability to sweep the ugly innuendos away and protect his woman ate at him. He'd expected scandal. But seeing the negative focus shift to Tori, with such snide inferences, sickened him.

His wonderful woman had been through so much.

Now, generously, she'd finally agreed to marry him for their son's sake. She'd signed on for a marriage without love, though it wasn't what she wanted. She'd agreed to learn a new way of life—not only in a country foreign to her, but as a royal, under constant scrutiny. He'd promised she wouldn't regret her decision.

And now... How could he ask this of her?

The answer was simple and terrible.

He couldn't.

Tori was on the floor with Oliver, watching his eyes grow round with excitement as, wobbling, he managed to stay sitting up before losing his balance and falling onto the cushion she'd put behind him.

Smiling at his achievement, and his delight, she was taken by surprise when Ashraf appeared.

'You're early.'

Pleasure filled her. All day she'd wondered if she'd done the sensible thing, agreeing to marry Ashraf. In the end she'd given up wondering if it was sensible, contenting herself with the fact that it was her only option if she wanted to be with the man she loved.

The glow inside her as she looked up at him told her she'd done right. Better to love than to turn her back on the chance of happiness.

'Gah-gah-gah.' Oliver, on his back, waved his arms and legs as he saw his father.

'Hello, little beetle.' Ashraf bent and scooped him up, lifting him high till Oliver crowed with excitement.

As ever, the sight of them together tugged at the sentimental cord that ran through her middle. It was stronger today, after she'd spent all night making glorious love to Ashraf.

Tori told herself that was why she felt emotional. Lack of sleep. *And finally admitting you're wildly in love with this man.*

'We need to talk.'

Ashraf looked down at her and that warm, squishy feeling solidified into a cold lump of concern. Something was wrong. She read it in the lines bracketing his mouth.

'Of course. I'll ring for the nanny.' Tori scrambled to her feet.

'No need. I've called her. Ah...' He turned at a knock on the door. 'Here she is.'

He took time to buss Oliver's cheek and let his son grab his fingers, all the while murmuring to him in his own language, before handing him to the nanny.

Finally they were alone. But Ashraf didn't pull Tori close. He didn't even take her hand, though when she'd last seen him he'd been reluctant to leave her bed. He'd lingered, stroking her hair, kissing her and murmuring endearments in a voice of rough suede that had made her feel maybe she was wrong. Maybe he might learn to love her one day.

Now, Ashraf didn't even look at her. He seemed fixated on the view from the window. His brow was pleated and his mouth was set so grimly that the back of her neck prickled in anticipation of bad news. Her stomach churned.

'What's wrong?' She came up beside him, put her hand on his arm then dropped it as he instantly stiffened. 'Ashraf?'

Tori had a really bad feeling now. During everything they'd been through never once had Ashraf shied away from her touch. Shock slammed her. It did no good telling herself that it wasn't revulsion she read in his grimace, even if the idea seemed crazy.

He turned but didn't reach for her. Instead he shoved his hands deep in his pockets, broad shoulders hunching. Tori felt his rejection like a punch to the solar plexus that sucked out her breath. What had happened to the tactile man who couldn't get enough of her?

'I'm sorry, Tori. I was distracted. Let's sit, shall we?'

She shook her head and planted her soles more firmly on the silk carpet. 'I'm fine here.' If it was bad news she'd rather have it standing up. 'Is it my father?'

'No, no. Nothing like that. There's no news from Australia.'

Tori's swift breath of relief surprised her. She didn't *like* her father but it seemed she did care for him at some level.

'So it's news from Za'daq?'

She looked into fathomless eyes and wished she knew what Ashraf was thinking.

Just when she thought he wasn't going to speak he took her hand, enfolding it in long fingers. Warmth trickled from his touch but dissipated with his words.

'I'll always treasure your generosity in agreeing to marry me, Victoria.'

For the first time the sound of Ashraf saying her full name sent a cold shiver through her—nothing like the shimmer of lush warmth it usually generated.

'But I'm freeing you from your promise.'

Tori felt his encircling hand tighten as she stumbled back, away from him, till finally she broke his hold.

'You don't want to marry me?'

In another time, another place, she'd have winced at the sound of her ragged voice. But it matched the way she felt. Off balance, as if someone had ripped that beautiful hand-woven rug from beneath her feet.

But the only ripping here was her heart. Her sad, foolish heart, which had opened itself up to Ashraf's kindness, strength and caring.

'I'm sorry.' He held her gaze, his own unwavering. 'It's for the best. I was selfish to ask you to give up your life and home and live in Za'daq. I see that now.'

Tori wanted to protest that living with him in Za'daq was what she craved, but he continued.

'As you wisely pointed out, Oliver will still have a family even if we live apart.'

Live apart.

Tori pressed her hand to the place below her ribs that felt hollow, as if an unseen hand had scraped out her insides. He didn't even want her in his country!

Out of the miasma of shock and hurt, indignation rose. 'That's not good enough.'

'Sorry?'

He'd obviously expected her simply to accept his decree. He wasn't the enlightened man she'd thought. All those generations of absolute rulers had left their mark. She read surprise in the lift of his eyebrows and determination in those haughty features.

'If you're going to jilt a woman you need to do better.'

For a second—a millisecond—she saw something pass across that set face. Then it was gone. If anything he stood straighter, imposing and rigid, like the soldier she'd discovered he'd once been. Or an autocrat looking down on a lesser being.

Yet even in her distress Tori couldn't believe that of Ashraf.

'Of course. I apologise. Again.'

He paused, and if she hadn't known better Tori would have said he was the one struggling for breath, not her.

'I should have started by saying I'm sorry for changing my mind.'

Changing his mind? Tori stared, incredulous. He wanted her to believe he'd simply *changed his mind*?

She shook her head, wrapping her arms around her middle to contain the empty feeling which threatened to spread and engulf her whole.

'Still not good enough, Ashraf. I need to know why.' A thought pierced her whirling brain. 'Is it someone else? Have you found a better bride?'

Someone local who understood Za'daqi ways. Some glamorous princess.

'Of course not!' He actually looked insulted.

'There's no "of course" about it.' Tori's voice grew in strength as anger masked pain. 'This morning, *in my bed*, you were happy with the arrangement. What changed?'

He winced and half turned away. Tori began to wonder if the caring, wonderful man she'd fallen in love with had been an illusion.

'You're right. You deserve to know.' He paused, breathing deep. 'The press, stirred by my opponents, have learned about Oliver. About us. The stories they're printing…' He spread his hands and grimaced. 'They're not to be borne. The filth they're spouting will only continue and I can't allow that. I have to stop it.'

'I see.'

It was clear from Ashraf's expression how important this was to him. Tori recalled his talk of past scandals, how he hadn't been accepted by the political elite, how he'd had to strive to win support for his schemes.

Was his situation so precarious? It seemed so. And so was the crown he wanted to pass to Oliver. Tori wanted to tell him that it didn't matter. That Oliver could make his way in the world without a royal title. But it did matter. This was Ashraf's birthright. He'd worked all his life to prove himself. Since becoming Sheikh he'd worked longer and harder than his predecessors to improve the nation. Tori had had that from Azia, who was forever singing Ashraf's praises.

This was his destiny. His purpose in life.

But that didn't stop her searing anguish as she faced facts. The man she loved was rejecting her because when it came to the crunch he, and his people, believed she wasn't good enough to stand at his side.

CHAPTER FOURTEEN

TORI TURNED AND marched away from the window into the shadows.

Ashraf wanted to follow and haul her close.

He didn't do it. If he touched her his good intentions would collapse and he wouldn't release her.

He swallowed and it felt as if he'd swallowed a desert of sand, his mouth so dry the action tore his throat to shreds.

This was the cost of releasing the one woman he'd ever cared for. *The one woman he could ever love.*

That, above all, gave him the strength to weld his feet to the floor.

He loved Tori. Loved her with such devotion that watching her struggle with his decision felt like the most difficult thing he'd ever done. Harder than facing the threat of death at Qadri's hands.

What would it be like, living the rest of his life without her?

The laceration in his throat became a raw ache that descended to his chest, intensifying to a sharper pain with each breath.

But he had to protect her. In his arrogance he'd assumed they'd face the scandal together. That it would be directed at *him*, with his notorious past, and that Tori would be seen as a victim of his licentious ways. He hadn't bargained on her being represented as some...

He frowned. Was that a sob?

Tori stood with her back to him, facing the courtyard. Her shoulders were straight but her head was bent. As he watched another quiver passed through her.

Seconds later he was behind her, hands lifted but not touching those slim shoulders. 'Tori, are you all right?'

Stupid question. Of course she wasn't. But how could he comfort her?

'Does it matter?'

Her steady voice made him feel, if possible, worse. 'It's my fault. I shouldn't have let this happen.'

'Which? Suggesting marriage or fathering Oliver?' She snorted. 'Don't answer that. Clearly you regret both.'

'No!' His fingers closed on her shoulders and he gritted his teeth, fighting the need to spin her round and into his arms. To hold her properly one last time. 'You can't think that.'

'There are a lot of things you control, Ashraf, but what I think isn't one of them.'

'Parting is for the best.' How he wished there were another way.

'Whose best? Yours? Not Oliver's or mine.' She shrugged from his hold and swung to face him.

Ashraf stared into eyes that glittered with tears she refused to let fall. For the first time he felt himself to be the failure his father had accused him of being.

The one woman in the world he wanted to protect from harm and he'd brought her infamy and scandal. The sight of her, brim-full with pain, knotted his conscience and stole his resolution.

'Don't lie, Ashraf. Just say it. It's too risky for your crown to take on a woman with a bastard son, even if you're his father.'

His breath hissed at the words and her eyes narrowed.

'That's it, isn't it?'

For a second she stood stock-still, eyes wide. He'd seen the victim of an accidental gunshot look exactly the same—that moment of disbelief before he crumpled to the ground. But Tori didn't crumple. She turned and stalked to the bedroom.

'It won't take me long to pack. We'll leave today.'

It was what he wanted. What was best for Tori. Yet Ashraf couldn't let her do it. He was too selfish.

'Wait!'

She kept walking, head up, shoulders back, but she stumbled as if she wasn't watching her step.

His heart twisted. 'Tori.'

'There's nothing to say.'

But there was. So much he barely knew where to start. He inserted himself between her and the bedroom door, frustrating her attempt to shove him aside.

'This isn't about me protecting my position—it's about protecting *you*.'

'You're not protecting me. You're banishing me.'

His heart, the organ he'd so long thought dormant, beat harder at the torment in her voice.

'If you're not here they'll focus on me, like they always have. You won't be a target.'

Silence. Silence that lasted so long he wondered if she were trying to freeze him out. Finally she blinked, like a sleepwalker rousing.

'The stories aren't about you?'

'Partly. But...'

But the most negative ones made it sound as if he'd fallen prey to some avaricious *femme fatale* who went through men like a fish through water.

'They focus on me, then,' she murmured. 'That makes sense. It makes you look bad and you can't afford that.'

Unable to stop himself, Ashraf grabbed her upper arms and pulled her close. 'How many times do I have to say it? I'm used to bad press. It's *you* I want to protect. You shouldn't have to put up with this.'

Her eyes rounded and she stopped trying to pull free. 'Are you serious?'

'Yes, I'm serious!'

He saw her blink and realised he'd raised his voice. It was something he never did. His father had shouted all the time when he was riled—at him, at servants, at inanimate objects.

Ashraf shuddered. Another sign he was losing control.

'Tell me what they're saying,' she said.

At first he refused, but Tori wore him down. When he'd finished she shook her head sadly and Ashraf knew he was right to send her away. If only he had the courage to do it.

'You'd really banish me so the press won't hound me?'

His chest rose high on a deep breath. 'It's not banishment. It's—'

'Sending me away from the man I love is banishment.' Her soft voice cut across his.

Everything inside Ashraf stilled. Even his pulse slowed, before speeding up to a gallop. He swallowed.

This time the sand in his throat had been replaced with a choking knot of tangling emotion.

'You don't love me.'

It was impossible. Even his mother hadn't loved him, choosing instead to run off with her paramour and leave Ashraf to her husband's mercy.

'Why don't I?'

Tori's smile trembled and his heart with it. He shook his head, unwilling to say the words. It was too big a risk. Yet perhaps for the first time in his life he needed to open himself up, though it made him even more vulnerable.

'Because I've never craved anything so much. And life's taught me never to expect such a blessing.'

'You poor, deluded man.'

Her palm covered his cheek and his eyelids drooped as the pent-up tension was expelled from his lungs. One touch, just one, did that.

'I've been in love with you more or less since we met.'

'That's crazy. You didn't know me.'

Yet he greedily hoarded each precious word. His hands firmed around her waist, pulling her closer.

'It was instinctive, and everything I believed about you has turned out to be right.' She frowned. 'Even down to your *managing* ways. Do you *really* think I'll curl up and die because the gutter press prints lies about me?'

'You shouldn't have to face that.'

Her chin lifted. 'You're right. I shouldn't. And I'm sure you and your lawyers will help me make them stop. But if you think I'm going to be scared away by gossip, think again.' Her mouth tilted at one corner. 'I work in a male-dominated industry. I've faced prejudice and sexual innuendo all my working life. Most of my peers are great, but there are always some who can't cope. I won't put up with it and I certainly won't let it destroy my happiness. Besides, I've learned a thing or two from my father about dealing with the press.'

Ashraf stared, stunned by the pragmatic courage of his beloved. He'd known she was special, yet still she surprised him.

'Ash?'

Her use of the old nickname was even more intimate than the feel of her hand on his flesh.

'You do want me?'

'Of course I do. I never want to let you go.'

He wrapped her tight in his arms. Not kissing her but simply embracing her. Feeling her heart beat against him, her breath a warm caress against his collarbone, her body a perfect fit to his.

Tori's uncertainty made heat prickle at the back of his eyes. His breath shuddered. He had a moment's recollection of feeling this close to tears only once before. He'd been about four and he'd often gone to play in the courtyard that had been his mother's. The garden's fragrance had reminded him of a long-ago comforting presence that he guessed must have been hers. But someone had told his father of his secret visits and he'd arrived to find all the scented roses pulled out. The place was a barren waste.

But Ashraf's palace wasn't barren. He had Tori—his woman, his lover, soon to be his wife. A heroine strong enough to stand beside him through whatever life held. And there was Oliver too.

'You do know,' he murmured, tilting her chin so he

could look into her glorious eyes, 'there's no turning back now.' His chest swelled with feelings he'd suppressed too long. 'I love you too much ever to let you go. If you get cold feet before the wedding I'll have the border closed and—'

'What? You'll kidnap me and ride off with me to your secret desert encampment? I like the sound of that.'

Her smile was wide and unshadowed. It seemed his Tori really had moved on from the trauma of their abduction.

Ashraf lowered his head so his mouth hovered above hers. 'I'd planned to honeymoon on my private island off the coast, but if you prefer the desert...'

'I prefer you kiss me and tell me again that you love me.'

He looked down, reading marvellous things in her gentle smile.

This. This was what he craved.

'Your wish,' he said against her lips, 'is my command.'

EPILOGUE

IT WAS A long wedding. Days long. Filled with good wishes, lavish entertainment, music, feasting and enough pomp to convince Tori that she really had married a king.

She returned to the audience chamber after freshening up to find Karim waiting for her, a query in his moss-green eyes. Beyond him the room was filled with guests in their finery, the air buzzing with animated conversation.

Funny to think she'd been wary about meeting Ashraf's brother. Everyone spoke of him in glowing terms and she'd wondered if it was true that he really didn't want Ashraf's crown. Till the brothers had told her their story and Karim had welcomed her into the family with genuine warmth.

His smile had been almost wistful as he'd admitted he'd never seen Ashraf so happy. That neither brother had expected to find true love. Tori's heart had squeezed at his words and she'd hugged him hard, eliciting mock protests from Ashraf and a quaintly clumsy hug from Karim. Clumsy, she suspected, because like Ashraf he wasn't used to emotional displays. It certainly couldn't be from lack of female companionship, for despite Karim being only his half-brother he shared Ashraf's chiselled good-looks and potent appeal.

'How are you holding up?' he asked.

Tori beamed at him. 'I'm doing well. Especially since everyone is so happy for us.'

Contrary to expectations, the ghastly rumours had ceased almost straight away when it turned out that the die-hards who disapproved of Ashraf were completely outnumbered by those who thought him an excellent Sheikh.

As for Oliver being born outside marriage—that didn't seem to be a problem now Ashraf had legitimised him. If anything, many Za'daqis viewed it as proof of their King's masculine potency and thought it natural that Tori had been swept off her feet. She'd discovered a strong romantic streak in his people.

'Ashraf sent me to find you.' Karim offered her his arm and when she curled her hand around it he bent to murmur in her ear. 'Unless you'd rather skip this bit and rest?'

She should be tired but Tori had never felt so energised. 'I wouldn't miss it for anything.'

'You don't even know what it is!'

Karim laughed as he steered her through the throng, his deep chuckle reminding her of Ashraf's. Even after a few days she knew that Karim, like her husband, rarely laughed aloud. Both were so serious, though Ashraf was learning to relax more.

'So tell me.'

They were outside now, on the terrace, looking down at the wide space where she'd previously watched horsemen and archers perform stunning feats of skill and bravery. Now the space was filled with people. More than filled. They spilled down the slope beyond into the public gardens and streets as far as the eye could see.

Tori stumbled to a halt. 'Where have they come from?'

A deep, familiar voice reached her.

'From everywhere—all across the country.'

It was Ashraf, his eyes shining. He looked magnificent in white robes trimmed with gold as he strode up and took her hands.

Tori's insides melted. Her Ashraf. Her husband.

Beside them Karim spoke. 'They're not VIPs, just ordinary people who've made their way here to wish you both well.' He clamped his hand on Ashraf's shoulder, leaning close and lowering his voice. 'You've done well, little brother. They love you.'

Ashraf shrugged, making little of the praise, though Tori saw that it moved him.

He turned to her. 'There's even a delegation from that first village I took you to in the foothills. Where you got that scarf.'

Tori looked down at the deep jewel colours of the scarf she'd teamed with a dress of vibrant teal, embroidered at the hem with silver. Over the last three days it seemed she'd worn every colour of the rainbow, and each time her pleasure in the magnificent wedding clothes was outshone by the appreciation in Ashraf's eyes.

'What are we waiting for? There are a lot of people to greet.'

Ashraf's slow smile made her heart drum faster.

'Thank you, *habibti*. It will mean a lot to them.' He looked at Karim. 'You'll come too, brother?'

Karim shook his head. 'This is your day—yours and Tori's. I'll go and deal with the VIPs.' He turned towards the palace, leaving Ashraf and Tori alone.

As Ashraf led her towards the expectant throng he tucked her close against him. 'I'm afraid this will add extra hours to the wedding celebrations. You'll need to rest when this is over.'

'It's not rest I need. I have other priorities.'

Ashraf stopped and turned to face her. 'Have I told you how very much I love you?'

His deep voice resonated and a ripple ran through the watching crowd.

'Yes.' She knew there were stars in her eyes as she looked up at him. 'But I never tire of hearing it.'

'And you love me.' His declaration was loud and proud.

'I do.'

The crowd cheered, and Ashraf grinned, and Tori knew she'd just embarked on the most remarkable, wonderful adventure of her life.

* * * * *

If you enjoyed
Sheikh's Royal Baby Revelation
by Annie West,
you're sure to enjoy these other
Secret Heirs of Billionaires stories!

Claimed for the Sheikh's Shock Son
by Carol Marinelli
Shock Heir for the King
by Clare Connelly
Demanding His Hidden Heir
by Jackie Ashenden
The Maid's Spanish Secret
by Dani Collins

Available now!

#3757 A PASSIONATE REUNION IN FIJI
Passion in Paradise
by Michelle Smart

Workaholic billionaire Massimo has convinced his estranged wife, Livia, to accompany him to Fiji. Trapped in paradise, an explosive reunion is in the cards, but only if their passion can burn away their past...

#3758 VIRGIN PRINCESS'S MARRIAGE DEBT
by Pippa Roscoe

At a Paris ball, Princess Sofia meets a man she never thought she'd see again—billionaire Theo. Now, as their chemistry reignites, Theo creates a scandal to finally claim Sofia's hand—in marriage!

#3759 THE INNOCENT'S EMERGENCY WEDDING
Conveniently Wed!
by Natalie Anderson

Katie can't believe she's asking notorious playboy Alessandro to marry her! It's only temporary, but when Alessandro tests the boundaries of their arrangement, untouched Katie finds herself awakened to unknown, but oh-so-tempting, desire...

#3760 DEMANDING HIS DESERT QUEEN
Royal Brides for Desert Brothers
by Annie West

Desert prince Karim needs a bride—and Queen Safiyah is the perfect choice. Yet the pain of their broken engagement years ago remains. Karim's demands are simple: a convenient marriage for their country's sake. Except Safiyah still fires his blood...

YOU CAN FIND MORE INFORMATION ON UPCOMING HARLEQUIN® TITLES, FREE EXCERPTS AND MORE AT WWW.HARLEQUIN.COM.

HPCNM0919RB

"Hiding away?" Livia asked.

"Taking a breather."

Dark brown eyes studied him, a combination of sympathy and amusement in them. Livia knew well how social situations made him feel.

She caught the barman's attention and ordered herself a bourbon, too. "This is a great party."

"People are enjoying it?"

"Very much." She nudged him with her elbow and pointed at one of the sofas. Two of the small children he'd almost tripped over earlier were fast asleep on it. A third, who'd gone a pale green color, was eating a large scoop of ice cream, utter determination etched on her face. "Someone needs to get that girl a sick bag."

He laughed and was immediately thrown back to his sister's wedding again.

He'd approached Livia at the bar. She'd said something inane that had made him laugh. He wished he could remember what it was but it had slipped away the moment she'd said it, his attention too transfixed on her for words to stick.

She'd blown him away.

Those same feelings...

Had they ever really left him?

The music had slowed in tempo. The dance floor had filled, the children making way for the adults.

"We should dance," he murmured.

Her chest rose, head tilted, teeth grazing over her bottom lip. "I suppose we should...for appearance's sake."

He breathed deeply and slowly held his hand out.

Equally slowly, she stretched hers out to meet his. The pads of her fingers pressed into his palm. Tingles shot through his skin. His fingers closed over them.

On the crowded dance floor, he placed his hands loosely on her hips. Her hands rested lightly on his shoulders. A delicate waft of her perfume filtered through his airwaves.

He clenched his jaw and purposely kept his gaze focused above her head.

They moved slowly in tempo with the music, their bodies a whisper away from touching…

"When did you take your tie off?" Livia murmured when she couldn't take the tension that had sprung between them any longer.

She'd been trying very hard not to breathe. Every inhalation sent Massimo's familiar musky heat and the citrus undertones of his cologne darting into her airwaves. Her skin vibrated with awareness, her senses uncoiling, tiny springs straining toward the man whose hands hardly touched her hips. She could feel the weight in them though, piercing through her skin.

Caramel eyes slowly drifted down to meet her gaze.

The music beating around them reduced to a burr.

The breath of space between them closed. The tips of her breasts brushed against the top of his flat stomach. The weight of his hands increased in pressure.

Heat pulsed deep in her pelvis.

Her hands crept without conscious thought over his shoulder blades. Heart beating hard, her fingers found his neck…her palms pressed against it.

His right hand caressed slowly up her back. She shivered at the darts of sensation rippling through her.

Distantly, she was aware the song they were dancing to had finished.

His left hand drew across her lower back and gradually pulled her so close their bodies became flush.

Her cheek pressed into his shoulder. She could feel the heavy thuds of his heart. They matched the beats of hers.

His mouth pressed into the top of her head. The warmth of his ragged breath whispered in the strands of her hair. Her lungs had stopped functioning. Not a hitch of air went into them.

A finger brushed a lock of her hair.

She closed her eyes.

The lock was caught and wound in his fingers.

She turned her cheek and pressed her mouth to his throat…

A body slammed into them. Words, foreign to her drumming ears but unmistakably words of apology, were gabbled.

They pulled apart.

There was a flash of bewilderment in Massimo's eyes she knew must be mirrored in hers before he blinked it away.

A song famous at parties all around the world was now playing. The floor was packed with bodies all joining in with the accompanying dance. Even the passed-out children had woken up to join in with it.

And she'd been oblivious. They both had.

Don't miss
A Passionate Reunion in Fiji.
Available October 2019 wherever
Harlequin® Presents books and ebooks are sold.

www.Harlequin.com